The Wounds of Life

M A R I O   M A R C O

PAGE PUBLISHING, INC.
Conneaut Lake, PA

First originally published by Page Publishing 2019

Based on a True Story
At the request of the survivors and family, the names and locations
have been changed.
Any resemblance to real persons, living or dead is purely
coincidental.

ISBN 978-1-64350-858-0 (pbk)
ISBN 978-1-64350-859-7 (digital)

Printed in the United States of America

CONTENTS

CHARACTERS

- Darius is the protagonist and narrator of the novel. He is originally from Iran but is forced to leave his country after a revolution. He struggles with his decision to leave his home country and the resulting death of his parents whom he had to leave behind.
- Sandee is the wife of Darius. Darius meets her while he is attending the University of Virginia. He eventually marries her and together they have two daughters, Artemisia and Farah Claire.
- Father Fredericks is an American missionary who inspires Darius to become a Christian.
- Matthew is the son Father Fredericks
- James is the son of Father Fredericks
- Artemisia is the first daughter of Darius and Sandee. She becomes a Virginia State Trooper, but her life is cut short after a car accident in which she is killed. The family struggles to cope with her loss.
- Farah Claire is the second daughter of Darius and Sandee. She meets and falls in love with Steve who becomes her husband and influences her to join the US Navy. She does and becomes a US Navy doctor, traveling with Doctors without Borders. She is deployed to Afghanistan and then eventually gets captured by Taliban fighters. Her ordeal is traumatic, but she survives and is eventually rescued by US Special Forces. Farah goes through changes as she returns back home a hero; but she struggles to cope with her injuries, rehabilitation, and PTSD. Eventually, she decides to

return to Afghanistan and sets up a nonprofit organization to help children and women of Afghanistan.

- Steve is a captain in the US Marines Corps who meets and falls in love with Farah Claire and eventual marries her.
- Moullah Mehsud is the leader of the Taliban. He has four wives: (1) Fatima, (2) Laila, (3) Bano Khno, and (4) Taban. Bano Khno is jealous of Moullah Mehsud's attraction to Farah Claire.
- Moullah Sardar is the son of Moullah Mehsud who takes an interest in the captured Farah Claire.
- Muhammad (son)
- Basiel Aziz (son)
- Noordin (son)
- Aziza (female)
- Darya (female)
- Nazanin (female)
- Fawzia (female)

PREFACE

◇◇◇

It was a cool, calm, and sunny day as Darius drove his car down the winding highway. He had gotten up really early this morning and dressed himself in his best clothing, a three-piece vested suit with a shiny bowtie. He also dressed Artemisia, his granddaughter, in her best clothing, a bright pink dress that she only wore on special occasions. Although they both ate breakfast together, Darius was unusually quiet.

After a while, they reached their destination, and Darius pulled the car up. Artemisia looked up as the car passed by a sign overhead that read: Virginia State Memorial Cemetery.

Darius quietly parked the car and asked Artemisia to follow him. They walked along a path until they came to a row of headstones. Artemisia didn't say anything; she just held her grandfather's hand. They stepped into a grassy area and walked farther. There were rows upon rows of neatly aligned headstones that could be seen all around as far as the eye could see. Each one had a different name, but the headstones were all the same size.

Then, Darius stopped. He let go of Artemisia's hand, knelt down on one knee at one of the headstones, touched it gently with his hand, and began to sob. He gently brushed his fingers along the letters engraved in the stone: A-R-T-E-M-I-S-I-A.

When he stopped crying, he gently took Artemisia's hand, and together, they both placed Persian Roses in a small holder located on the headstone. Earlier that day, Darius had cut the roses along with some jasmine that he received from his home country of Iran. These were very symbolic to him because they brought back good memories of a time when Darius was home—back to a time and place when his family was together, at peace.

After a few minutes of silence, Darius stood up, took Artemisia's hand, and they walked over to a bench next to the gravesite and sat down. Then, with tears in his eyes and a trembling voice, Darius looked directly into Artemisia's small eyes and said, "Today is the twenty third of March. It is the first day of spring, and it is also the Persian New Year. I brought you hear today because I need to tell you an important story. It is a story about me, about our family, and about your great-aunt and your beautiful mother, and your aunt Artemisia."

> *I turn to right and left, in all the earth*
> *I see no signs of justice, sense, or worth;*
> *A man does evil deeds, and all his days*
> *Are filled with luck and universal praise;*
> *Another's good in all he does—he dies*
> *A wretched, broken man whom all despise.*
> *—THE PERSIAN BOOK OF KINGS*

INTRODUCTION

"In my experience, men who respond to good
fortune with modesty and kindness are harder to
find than those who face adversity with courage."
—Cyrus the Great King of Persia

This is a story about an Iranian college student during the war
between Iran and Iraq in 1980. Because of the war, he was forced to
leave his country and pursue happiness, a better life, and religious
freedom so that he could practice his love of Christianity, which was
introduced to him by an American missionary, Father Fredericks,
back in 1978 and 1979 in Tehran, Iran.

In his quest for his freedom, Darius comes to the United States
and eventually ends up residing in the state of North Virginia. There,
he finds the freedom to continue with his education and become a
good doctor and heart surgeon. He also discovers his beloved wife,
Sandee. She becomes his best friend and colleague, and after one year
they get married. They eventually have two daughters, Artemisia and
Farah Claire. One becomes a Virginia State Trooper, and the other
becomes a U. S. Navy medical officer who serves in Afghanistan.

This is also a story about one family and their two daughters
and the many obstacles they encounter and eventually overcome.
First, Darius is forced to leave his beloved country of Iran after it is
hurled into a turbulent revolution. Second, Darius struggles with his
decision to become a Christian after meeting Father Fredericks and
tries to cope with the loss of his parents whom he left behind in Iran
and who later die. Then, Darius meets and falls in love with Sandee.
They eventually get married and have two children, Artemisia and

9

Farah Claire. Both grow up to be very successful. Unfortunately, Artemisia is killed unexpectedly in a car accident, and this leaves the family struggling to find a way to cope with the loss. Once again, Darius finds that his faith is being tested with the loss of a loved one.

Farah Claire meets and falls in love with Steve, who is a US Marine Corps Captain when they first meet. Eventually, they decide to become a married couple and make plans for a future life together as husband and wife. Unfortunately, Farah Claire is deployed to Afghanistan, and her story takes a somber turn after she is captured by Taliban fighters. Farah struggles to regain her freedom from her captors and ultimately is rescued but not before being wounded and beaten and intimately involved in a love triangle between two powerful warlords, Moullah Mehsud and his son, Moullah Sardar. Both become infatuated with Farah Claire, and they want to exploit her for their own purposes: one to use her as a means to get a healthy ransom, the other to use her as his own slave.

Farah Claire is rescued from the enemy's hands and thus begins the long work of healing and recovery. Despite her ordeal, she makes plans to return back to Afghanistan. Her hope is to be able to make a difference in the lives of the women and children there so that they can experience the joy of freedom and self-independence.

CHAPTER 1

<<<<<<<<<<<<<<<<<<<<<<<<<<<<<<<<<<<<<<<<<<<<<<<<<<<<<<<<<<

The Saga Begins

"It does not matter how slowly you go as long as
you do not stop."

My name is Darius. I was a young college student during the
Iran revolution back in 1979. It feels like it was yesterday when I left
my beloved country. I remember there was chaos everywhere. People
were angry about the revolution and did not know where to go or
how to fix the turmoil. Many people wondered: "where is the Shah
of Iran? I guess everybody forgot about our country."

There was a time, not long ago, when Iran used to be best
friends with the United States and Israel. What happened to us? Why
all of a sudden nobody likes us? I don't know. So many unanswered
questions. All I know is that things changed ... abruptly.

Maybe it was all a mistake, maybe it wasn't? Some people believed
it was all orchestrated by the US President Jimmy Carter because he
did not like the Shah of Iran (Iranian king). Some believed it was
because the Shah was speaking out publicly about the price of oil
possibly going up in OPEC. OPEC is the Organization of Petroleum
Exporting Countries, that was founded at a meeting on September
14, 1960, in Baghdad, Iraq. It had five founding members: Iran,
Iraq, Kuwait, Saudi Arabia, and Venezuela.

Still, others believe that too many people had been negatively
affected by the Shah's White Revolution, an ambitious program of

reforms to divide landholdings such as those owned by religious foundations, that grant women the right to vote and equality in marriage and allow religious minorities a greater share in governmental offices.

From 1941 until 1979, Iran was ruled by a constitutional monarchy under Mohammad Reza Pahlavi, Iran's Shah (king).

Although Iran, also called Persia, was the world's oldest empire, dating back 2,500 years, by 1900, it was floundering. Bandits dominated the land; literacy was 1 percent; and women, under archaic Islamic dictates, had no rights.

The Shah changed all this. Primarily by using oil-generated wealth, he modernized the nation. He built rural roads, postal services, libraries, and electrical installations. He constructed dams to irrigate Iran's arid land, making the country 90 percent self-sufficient in food production. He established colleges and universities and, at his own expense, set up an educational foundation to train students for Iran's future.

Yet despite all of these unprecedented achievements, in January of 1979, political unrest and declining health, forced the Shah to leave Iran. His sister felt that the best doctors were in the United States. When they applied for asylum, he was denied by the Carter administration. The U.S. President Jimmy Carter, ultimately" orchestrated the removal of the Shah from Iran and put him into exile.

Shortly afterward, the Shah was overthrown. The new regime, under the direction of the Islamic extremist Ayatollah Khomeini, then set to work reversing every pro-western policy of the Shah's government, such as women's rights and the citizenry's access to western media.

Khomeini was allowed to seize power in Iran. As a result, we are now reaping the harvest of anti-American fanaticism and extremism. Khomeini unleashed the hybrid of Islam and Marxism that has spawned suicide bombers and hijackers. President Jimmy Carter and the extremists in his administration, are to blame and should be held accountable.

CHAPTER 2

<hr/>

Father Fredericks:
A Meeting with Destiny

"Always bear in mind that your own resolution
to succeed is more important than any other."

It was during this period of revolution in my country that I met
Father Fredericks. He was an American missionary priest assigned to
Tehran, Iran. We met accidentally in a Tehran teahouse shop while I
was waiting for a table, so I could sit down and drink some Persian
tea. While we were standing in line, Father Fredericks started a conversation with me about the revolution and why people were upris-
ing and other topics. In the meantime, we got a table for two, and I
invited Father Fredericks to sit down and talk more because I became
curious about him and wondered what he was doing in Iran.

I felt amazed to be able to speak to a foreigner from such a distant land. Father Fredericks was a kind gentleman and a good priest.
He told me about Jesus Christ and the suffering of his people and
about freedom of all religions. Afterward, he asked me if I have time
for some charity work at the church. Of course, I said I would be
happy to help out.

So the next day, I met Father Fredericks at his church, along
with his wife and two children. Surprisingly, his wife was Iranian and

a very kind lady. Her name was Roya, and they had two beautiful sons, James and Matthew.

While we were working in the church, we heard chaos outside and the sound of cheering and chanting "death to the Shah." People were out in large crowds in the street protesting and throwing stones at the soldiers and policemen. The police and soldiers responded by pepper spraying and throwing smoke canisters at the protesters.

Because the church was in the vicinity of the area, some of the protesters ran into the church. The police were after them. Father Fredericks let everybody into the church. Then, he stood at the front door and spoke to the policemen kindly, saying, "This is a house of God. Please leave at once. This is no place for violence." To everyone's astonishment, the policemen accepted that explanation and left the area quietly. Then, we started helping all of the people that came into the church.

Shortly after that, there was a revolution, and unfortunately, the majority of foreigners, including Father Fredericks and his family, had to leave our country. Of course, this caused me great sorrow and sadness. What hurt me the most, was that I didn't even get a chance to say goodbye to Father Fredericks or his beautiful family because it was very difficult to travel anywhere at the time. However, Father Fredericks did manage to leave me a handwritten note. The note simply said, "Darius, remember, always stay rooted in faith."

Despite Father Fredericks not being around, I still studied my Bible that Father Fredericks had given to me. It had become something that I always cherished, and I would diligently read it word by word, especially when things would go wrong. In it, I found strength, peace, and a sense of purpose.

CHAPTER 3

Attack of the US Embassy in Iran

"Happiness is not something readymade. It comes from your own actions."

Not long after Father Fredericks departed Iran, some students and people from all ages and walks of life attacked the U.S. Embassy in Tehran, taking all employees hostage. I later learned that this was being guided by the new regime at the time. On almost every television, you could see the rioters attacking the U.S. Embassy, taking all of the diplomats and personnel in the embassy hostage. They were demanding the return of the Shah, so that he could face judgment in the Islamic regime court. Later, they changed their tone, declaring that it was the U.S. Embassy who was spying on the Iranian Islamic Regime. What a disaster. All I kept thinking at the time, was how could we do such terrible things. Of course, everyone was very worried that America might attack Iran as soon as possible because we did such a horrible act. No attack ever came, but the U.S. President Jimmy Carter orchestrated a rescue mission. Unfortunately, it failed miserably, and the hostages were left to linger in limbo.

Carter abandoned the Shah, and his United Nations ambassador went so far as to call the Ayatollah Khomeini "some kind of saint." The Shah went into exile, but Carter refused to allow him into the U.S. until the Shah became mortally ill. The mullahs demanded that Carter hand the Shah. Carter wouldn't do that, but he wanted him out. Iranian fury at the U.S. rose, and in 1979, hostages were taken at the American embassy in Tehran. (Shortly thereafter the Shah left, ending up in Egypt, where he died.) Carter was now engulfed in the Iranian hostage crisis, the first in a series of American clashes with the Iranian mullahs that would continue straight through to today. Notably, those who insist that America would be better off if Saddam Hussein had remained in power never get around to making the same claim for the Shah. But in the wake of his overthrow, a country that was once a solid American ally went in the hands of the Ayatollah and radical mullahs and mobs. This has affected the foreign policy of every one of Carter's successors, resulting in another hostage crisis (in Lebanon), the murder of Marines in their Beirut barracks, the hijacking of TWA flight 847, and the murder of passenger and US Navy diver Robert Stethem. All of these involved Hezbollah or the Islamic Jihad or both. And both were financed by the new Islamic masters of Iran.

CHAPTER 4

<><><><><><><><><><><><><><><><><><><><><><><><><><><><><><><><><><><><><><><><>

Iran–Iraq War:
The Beginning of the End

"There are no short cuts to any place worth going."

In the meantime, all of the colleges closed, and we could not go to classes. Over one year later, all of the hostages were freed. Unfortunately, on September 22nd, Iraq launched a surprised military attack on Iran. We were sleeping, when suddenly we heard many explosions. We did not know what was happening to us. All you could hear outside was the sounds of sirens, and pa speakers, telling us to get to safety. So many people died on that day, and there was no answer or reason for the attack. What an agony and a disaster to happen to us.

I still shiver when I recall all of the terrible events of that day, screaming, explosions, terror, widespread fear, and ... death. It is something I shall never forget.

On September 22nd, 1980, Iraq launched a surprise military attack on Iran, thereby igniting a war that would last for eight years, ending only when both countries agreed to accept the terms of a United Nations (UN) cease-fire resolution. Iraq's stated reason for initiating the war was defensive: The government in Baghdad claimed that Iranian forces were staging raids across their common border and that Iran's leaders were using the media to incite Iraqis to revolt. But Iraq had experienced more serious "border incidents" with Iran in the past, most notably in the years 1971–1975, when the regime of Mohammad Reza Shah Pahlavi had provided well-publicized "covert" assistance for a rebellion among Iraq's Kurdish minority. The same Iraqi leaders who were determined to avoid major conflict with Iran in 1975 had become, only five years later, confident of defeating Iran in battle. The Iraqi perception of changes in international, regional, and domestic politics contributed importantly to the decision to invade a larger and more powerful neighbor.

In the fall of 1980, Iran was isolated internationally as a result of the hostage crisis with the United States. Iran's relations with the other superpower, the Soviet Union, also were problematic because Tehran opposed the Soviet role in Afghanistan. In addition, all the Arab neighbors of Iran shared Iraq's apprehensions about the Iranian rhetoric of "exporting Islamic revolution." Within Iraq, Iran's revolution had emboldened an antigovernment movement among some Shi'ite Muslims, although the actual extent of this opposition may have been exaggerated in the minds of officials. Finally, intelligence about Iran supplied by Iranian military officers who had fled their country in the wake of the 1979 revolution was replete with information about serious factional rivalries among the political leaders and disarray and demoralization within the armed forces. The combined weight of all these factors persuaded Iraqi leaders that war against Iran could be undertaken with minimal costs and major potential benefits, such as seriously weakening or even causing the downfall of a much-distrusted regime.

Initially the war went well for Iraq. Iranian forces were surprised by and unprepared for the attack. Iraqis captured Iranian border towns in all four provinces adjacent to Iraq, as well as Iran's major port, Khorramshahr. The Iraqis also besieged Abadan, one of Iran's largest cities and the site of its largest oil refinery and several smaller cities located 12 to 20 miles removed from the border. After several weeks, however, the Iranians recovered from the shock of invasion and mobilized a large volunteer army that stopped the Iraqi advance. Iraq offered a cease-fire in place, which Iran rejected on grounds that part of its territory was under enemy occupation. For the next six months, the two armies fought intermittent battles along the front line in the western part of the Iranian province of Khuzestan, with neither side achieving any significant victory. Beginning in mid-1981, however, the Iranians gradually gained an advantage, breaking the Iraqi siege of several cities, including Abadan in September. A major victory for Iran came in May 1982, when it recaptured Khorramshahr. Several weeks later, in response to Israel's invasion of Lebanon, Iraq announced its forces would withdraw from all Iranian territory.

The summer of 1982 seemed an appropriate time to end the war, but Iran's leaders were beginning to feel victorious and wanted revenge. Thus, in July they decided to continue the war by taking it into Iraq. During the next five years, the advantage in the land battles on the Iraqi front remained with Iran, although it was an advantage that gained Iran only a few miles of ground, notably the Majnun Islands in 1984 and the Fao Peninsula in 1986. Strategy in this period may be described as a war of attrition; thousands of men, especially on the Iranian side, which used human wave assaults as a tactic, died in battles that ended as stalemates. In the air, the advantage was on Iraq's side, and the latter used its superiority in aircraft and missiles to strike at Iran's oil installations, industrial plants, shipping, and cities. Iraq also began to use chemical weapons against Iranian forces. Baghdad even authorized the use of chemical weapons against its own Kurdish minority in northeastern Iraq after some of them rebelled and provided logistical support to Iran.

Iraqi missile and aerial bombing of Iranian oil shipping led Iran to retaliate against the shipping of neutral Arab states, such as Kuwait, which Iran accused of collaborating with Iraq by providing billions of dollars in loans. The result was the "tanker war" in the Persian Gulf, a phase that added an international dimension to the war when major countries intervened during 1987 to assert the freedom of the seas by sending armed naval ships to escort neutral vessels through Gulf waters. The situation prompted the United Nations Security Council to pass a cease-fire resolution (1987). Iran initially was reluctant to accept this resolution, but a combination of factors finally secured its acceptance: Iraq's extensive use of chemical weapons in battles during early 1988; a renewed wave of Iraqi missile strikes on Iranian cities, including the capital, Tehran; an increasing war-weariness among the general population; and an uncertainty about the intentions of the United States and other countries that had intervened to suppress the tanker war. The UN-mediated cease-fire came into effect in August 1988. By that time, Iran had lost 150,000 men in battle, and about 40,000 more were listed as missing in action; 2,000 Iranian civilians also had been killed in Iraqi bomb and missile strikes. Iraq had lost more than 60,000 men in battle, and at least 6,000 Iraqi Kurdish civilians had been killed by chemical weapons unleashed on them by their own government.

CHAPTER 5

<><><><><><><><><><><><><><><><><><><><><><><><><><><><><><><><><><><>

Jail and Torture

"A broken hand works, but not a broken heart"

Not long after Father Fredericks and his family left, I was going outside to buy some bread for my family. Along the way to the store, I heard somebody calling my name. I looked back, and then all I remember was somebody putting something over my head. They said, "You are coming with us," and I replied, "What are you doing? You cannot do this!" Then I felt pain and shock through my entire body, and I collapsed. I later learned that I had been shocked with an electric baton. It felt as if I was dying.

When I opened my eyes, I found myself inside the notorious Islamic regime jail (Evin). I immediately recognized one of the jailers. He was one of my neighbors. His name was Majid. So I asked him, "Why am I here?" and he said with a hostile voice, "Shut up, you converted from the Muslim religion. We know about you. Why did you become a Christian? What is wrong with you? Don't you realize that it brings shame to our religion and our country and the Islamic regime and your family? We are going to teach you a lesson. You are going to find out what the Islamic regime means."

I was utterly shocked. But after a few minutes, I replied and said, "I am a free man. I can choose whatever I like to do, and you cannot do anything to me to change my mind. I just want to be a good Christian person." With that said, several guards approached me and began repeatedly hitting me with batons until I passed out. This was the beginning of my captivity.

Sometime much later, I found out that the sister of the jailer was at my home helping my mother for some Islamic charity. She accidently walked into my room and saw two posters of Jesus spread across one of my walls. That is how the jailer found out that I was a convert to Christianity. Of course, I couldn't help but wonder "is this my reward for becoming a Christian? Is this how it's going to be from now on?"

CHAPTER 6

<><><><><><><><><><><><><><><><><><><><><><><><><><><><><><><><><><>

Life in Evin Prison

"The best memory is that which forget nothing,
but injuries. Write kindness in marble, and write
injuries in the dust."

It is known as Evin University, but it's no school, it is one of the world's most brutal and infamous prisons. Beatings, torture, mock executions, and brutal interrogations are the norm at Evin prison, where for decades the anguished cries of prisoners have been swallowed up by the drab walls of the low-slung lockup in northwestern Tehran. Standing at the foot of the Alborz Mountains, it is home to an estimated fifteen thousand inmates, including killers, thieves, and rapists. But the prison has also held ayatollahs, journalists, intellectuals, and dissidents over the years; and few if any who have survived time in Evin, would be surprised by claims of torture and abuse made by Abedini's supporters.

To many Iranians, the concept of Evin prison is synonymous with political repression and torture.

Today, anyone who is perceived to be a threat to the Iranian regime, including human rights defenders are kept within the confines of Evin and other notorious prisons in Iran.

Evin House of Detention was built during the reign of Mohammad Reza Pahlavi, known to Americans as the Shah of Iran. Before he was ousted from power in the 1979 revolution, the prison housed some of the very radicals and sympathizers who would one day rule the Islamic Republic. During the ten-year reign of Ayatollah Ruhollah Khomeini, thousands of political prisoners were systematically murdered at Evin. After Khomeini's death in 1989, Evin continued to serve as a holding pen for some of Iran's most prominent intellectuals, activists, and journalists, earning it the nickname Evin University.

Following Mahmoud Ahmadinejad's election as president in 2005, arrests related to political opposition mounted, reaching a frightening apex during the failed "Green Revolution" that followed Ahmadinejad's disputed 2009 reelection.

Darius's life was limited to interrogations. He would be blindfolded and taken to the interrogation room every morning to mock his belief. They would say things like "You are foolish to have converted to Christianity", and "We have arrested Jesus Christ, he is in the other cell". Darius knew that if he was released, he would have no choice, but to flee to Turkey, and ultimately immigrate to the United States.

CHAPTER 7

Released but not Free

"In the hour of adversity be not without hope for crystal rain falls from black clouds."

After several months of captivity, it was my family that came to my rescue. They were able to put some money aside and made a promise to the government religious police that I would be a good Muslim. It was only then that I was released.

Not too long after my release, I received a letter from the Islamic government stating that they needed me to join the fight for the Islamic regime. It said that they wanted me to join in as soon as possible. I wondered, "What do we do now? My country is in chaos. Everywhere government spies say they can put you in jail for any reason. Why does this happen to us? Why can no one answer me?" Everybody kept telling me to "keep quiet, don't say anything, be a good Muslim, and follow the rules." However, for me this just didn't seem right. And, of course, it is not in my nature to just go along with the flow, act as if everything is okay when things clearly were not. I have so many questions. For example, why in the name of God do we have to kill others if we are good Muslims? Also, I wondered why do we have to kill other Muslims. Of course, as usual, no one had any reasonable answers for these types of questions. Perhaps it was because most people lived in fear, fear of being abducted, fear of being persecuted, fear of being arrested, and fear of being beaten or tortured or even killed. Yet I could not understand how people could just accept the status quo and never do anything to change their circumstances. I wanted things to change for the better.

After several days of freedom, my cousin called me. He said, "Cousin, do not come out to the streets because the government is taking all young people sixteen years and above to nearby military bases. They want them to become soldiers and head to the front lines for the war against our neighbor, Iraq."

Of course, by this time, my parents had become deeply worried for me because they knew about my ideology and they knew that I was not going to change my mind about my love for Jesus Christ and about being a good Christian. So they sold lots of belongings and one of their houses to get the money that they handed to me saying, "Son, please leave this country as soon as possible. We are going to help you by sending you to your grandparent's village up to the northern border of Turkey." Of course, I was shocked, feeling sad and crying. I was also very angry. I felt that I didn't do anything wrong. Yet because of what I believe in, my family was making me leave the country. And so came the moment when my father, with sincerity and concern in his eyes, said, "Son, please don't make it any more difficult for us than it already is."

"I want to stay. I want to be with my family," I screamed. My dad simply responded by saying, "Son, there is no future for you here. Only war and blood. And as you know, this government is looking for you. Please go." So, with much resignation, I agreed to leave the only home that I've ever known. Little did I know what was in store for me in the days and months ahead. Everything was in chaos … and my life as I knew it was being turned upside down.

CHAPTER 8

Exodus from Iran (First Attempt)

(BY DARIUS)

"When the tide of misfortune moves over you,
even jelly will break your teeth."

I remember my time spent in Evin. It was a period of intense fear, uncertainty, and brutal torture at the hands of my own countrymen. I really thought that I was going to die there. I think that's when I realized that I would have to leave my beloved country. So after I was released, I went underground and disappeared.

Shortly after I left my hometown, the Islamic regime was looking for me everywhere, but I was nowhere to be found. Instead, I was hiding out in my grandmother's basement, in a different part of the town.

My family was still very worried about my safety. So they contacted some of our other family members in the city of Tabriz for help. Unfortunately, they refused to help me because they were afraid that they themselves would be persecuted for giving a safe house to a converted man from Muslim to Christianity. In the meantime, I was on the run.

At times, I was sleeping in the jungle and in parks or underneath bridges. I looked like a homeless person. Once in a while, I contacted my family or sent them notes to tell them that I was okay. Finally, one day, I met my father, and he gave me some money. He wanted me to leave the country and forget about the family. He said, "When you get to the safe area, please call us." My heart was in turmoil; should I go or should I stay. In the end, I decided to leave, despite my reservations and concerns for the safety of my parents.

Even though it was extremely difficult and scary at the time to get from one city to the other due to checkpoints, I managed to hitch-hike my way to the northern part of Iran. Sometimes, along the way, I would see young men being taken away from their families by force so that they could join the war against Iraq. Since most people traveled by bus, it was not uncommon for the regime soldiers to stop the bus, force the young men to get off the bus, oftentimes shouting, "We need you for the regime. We are fighting against nonbelievers. Islam is in danger. You must do your part for Allah and our leader Khomeini. You have to join the cause and fight for Islam." Many times I saw families begging the regime soldiers to spare their sons. "Please stop this. He is a student, or he is my only son," they would say. Sadly, the regime soldiers ignored everyone's pleas and continued to round up every young man and put them all into military trucks. On many occasions, the mothers of the sons would hold on to their loved ones, trying in desperation not to let go as they were being dragged away. It was such a horrific sight to see. Of course, the regime soldiers would respond by hitting the mothers with batons and even firing shots with pistols into the air to intimidate everyone. In the end, they got their way.

Eventually, I reached the northern border of Iran called Bazargan. When I arrived, I met some people with the same problems and asked them for help in crossing the border. We found a Kurdish-Iranian human smuggler. After a week, we moved to a nearby village and were introduced to another group of travelers. All of us wanted to get out of the country because it had become unsafe, especially for those who had converted to another religion.

I paid a smuggler four hundred dollars to transport me in the back of a fruit truck to the Turkish border. I was crammed in with fifty other Iranian exiles from all walks of life, which included women and children. Together we were crammed into a windowless container. I and the others were soon dropped off about five miles from the border.

The entire group was camped in a field waiting for the smuggler's to help us cross the border. However, several men armed with pistols and assault rifles stormed in and robbed everybody of their cash and backpacks. An hour later, as the scared group huddled in the field, the Iranian Islamic Police Border burst into the camp and arrested everyone.

They were yelling at us, "You are using this road to go to Turkey so you can join Western non-believers. We are going to teach you a lesson."

We were telling them, "No, we want to flee." They did not listen.

Everyone in the group was tied up and beaten. We were then shuffled from prison to prison, including one that housed what I estimated to be at least two thousand other Iranians at the time who also had been arrested for trying to cross into Turkey. During the day, other prisoners and I were forced to work in the homes of Iranian Islamic Regime police.

They were forcing us to do chores, like washing their cars, cleaning their houses, cleaning their backyard. And if anyone resisted, they came and beat that person badly.

Later we found out that several other groups were fatally shot when the group was intercepted by Iranian Islamic Revolutionary police guards.

I was humiliated. They had large clubs in their hands and basically acted like they were shepherds and we were flocks of animals.

One of my great-uncles was able to eventually convince and bribe one of the Islamic Regime Moullahs who had lots of influence in the area at the time. So he was able to temporarily release me. I still don't know what happened to the others in our group. In the meantime, I was not supposed to leave the city until my case went to court. So I had to wait.

CHAPTER 9

Exodus from Iran: Freedom
(Second Attempt)

"Where we love is home—home that our feet
may leave, but not our hearts."

With the little money that I did have, I was able to bribe one of
the regime jailers and get a message to my uncle. I requested his help
to get me out of jail.

Eventually my uncle came to my rescue. He gave me money,
which I used to contact another famous smuggler who was well-
known in the area. So I was able to be released.

After several weeks of searching for another smuggler, I was
finally able to find someone who could help. There were many spies
and other government regime individuals who were looking for people trying to flee the country so that they can turn them into the
government for rewards. Finally, I met someone who I could trust.
This allowed me to make a second attempt at escape.

I was introduced to a group of Iranian exiles. Among them
there were senators, doctors, lawyers, politicians, scholars, and others simply wanting to leave the country. Some had family and some
were without. You can imagine that nobody trusted anyone. We were
only allowed to go out at night to use the restroom or smoke. After
about two months, finally, the day had arrived for us to make another

move. Raza, the smuggler, came to us and he said, "Tonight, we are leaving. You have to travel light and fast, also you have to be vigilant and quiet. We are leaving in one hour."

About two in the morning, we left the village. Raza introduced us to a shepherd. He mixed us in with cows and sheep and goats. He gave us dressings of animal clothing, and he told us when we get to the nearby outpost at the Iranian border that we would have to wear these dressings of animal clothing and walk like a sheep. This is the only way to pass the border, he said. Another thing that helped was that we had children with us. When the shepherd saw that our group had women and children, he took great sympathy on us, and he decided to take us on a much farther journey. So the shepherd guided us to the far side of the border so that we could pass through. After several kilometers, we reached an area of barb-wire fence. So we have to cut it up. We had to wait for about forty-five minutes to cut the barbwire. As we struggled to get through the barbwire fence, in the distance we could hear many explosions. We learned later that it was landmines that the Islamic regime police had set up as traps in order to prevent people from leaving the country. Finally, after what seemed like an eternity, we made it.

In the distance, we saw a flashlight. That was the other person from the Turkish side of the border. Upon reaching him, all of us traveled to a nearby village on the Turkish side of the border and camped out in an abandoned barnyard. As soon as the shepherd told us all that we could rest, we all found a place on the ground and slept among all of the animals. It had been over sixteen hours since we started our journey and everyone was exhausted. We all fell asleep quickly without even thinking about what is going to happen to us.

When the next morning arrived, someone came with some bread and cheese and water and told us to stay here until midnight. Around 4:00 AM, we all could hear the sound of a noisy engine. Then, someone opened the door of the barnyard, entered cautiously, and told us to hurry up and get outside to the bus. On the way, I was looking into the other people's faces, which I could not see clearly until this point. Everyone was scared, including me. I'm sure everyone was thinking that something bad was going happen. Tension gripped the air like a tightrope.

The bus drove us to a nearby train station. At the train station, we got onboard a train that was heading for Istanbul. Once we arrived at the city, we met many other Iranians. However, everyone knew that we had only one hope—to get safely to any European country, the United States, or Canada as soon as possible. If we were captured along the way, it would surely be death for us all.

In the meantime, I was looking for a public phone because I wanted to make a phone call to my parents. I just wanted to let them know that I was well and had made it safely to Turkey. I was looking for my money and my wallet, but it was nowhere to be found. That's when I realized that someone had robbed me. "Welcome to Istanbul," I said to myself. Then I panicked. "Oh my god, how can I buy anything or go anywhere? How do I contact my family? I have no money." Then I heard someone saying, "Hey, let's go to the United Nations office. I heard that many Iranians are going there to get help. Let's go. It is not too far from here. I am sure they are able to help us." So, without any hesitation, we followed that person until we got to the United Nations office.

When we arrived at the United Nations office, we saw thousands upon thousands of people gathered together in line. Many were shouting, "We need help. Please help us to get to our destination. Open your hearts to us—we are in the war. We lost everything, we've been forced to leave our country. How can you forget us?" When I saw and heard these cries for help, I was deeply devastated and saddened. I began to cry and sob. Suddenly, a loud voice came over the intercom, and it said, "All Iranians who have the ability to speak or translate English, please come forward. See the officer in front. We need your assistance." So without any hesitation, I found myself walking to the front of the gate. I wiped my eyes clearly and strongly told the officer, "I can help. Please let me in."

The officer responded and said, "Okay, please come with me." As I was about to be taken through the gate, two small children and their mother grabbed him by both arms. They began to cry and plead for his help. "Look into your heart. We've been here for several months. We are stranded. We are out of food and out of money, and we need urgent help. Please help us to get to the United States. We have family, and they will reward you for your help." I smiled and said in a calm voice, "Don't worry, I will help you." Then I walked through the gate and into the United Nations office.

I was taken to a room filled with hundreds of people waiting for instruction from UN personnel. They were asking for people that knew English to help out with forms and other administrative needs. Of course, I offered to help. After a small briefing on what to do, myself and others started getting the forms filled out and showing other people how to fill out the applications and information on the forms. It was such a relief to finally be someplace where people actually cared about you. Thank God for their help because I did not know how we would have survived. However, even though I was now safe, I was deeply worried about my family that I had left behind.

After several hours, some United Nations and Red Cross personnel came out and announced that everyone would be put into different groups and guided by UN personnel to a nearby hotel that had been rented for refugees and immigrants. It had been set up especially for those refugees and immigrants who had been affected by the war between Iran and Iraq. Everyone would be given food assistance, clothing, hygiene items, and money. "In the meantime, we are going to process your requests but we ask for your patience," one of them said.

When we made it to the hotel, the United Nations along with Red Cross personnel handed everyone some money and some food and told us, "Please don't worry about anything. We are going to help you. If you need anything, please contact the United Nations' and Red Cross's toll free numbers on the paper we are giving you."

After several months, and with a lot of prayer, I received the good news, my application was accepted and I was officially given a visa to go to the United States as a refugee.

CHAPTER 10

The Price of Freedom:
Casualties of War

"Nothing is easy in war. Mistakes are always paid
for in casualties."

I settled in my new surroundings in Virginia. And after a warm welcome from US officials and others, finally I was able to make a phone call to my family.

When my mother picked up the phone, I knew something was wrong just by the tone of her voice. I asked her about my father, and she became quiet. Then I pleaded with my mother and I said "Please, where is my dad?" I could hear my mother begin to cry. She said "Son, after you left the country, the government regime revolutionary guards were looking for you. Since they couldn't find you, they abducted your father and put him in jail for seven months. Afterwards, he was released, but then they made him join the civilian military. Eventually, they sent him to the front lines of war. The only thing that kept your father going strong was that he knew somehow you were safe, and no one can harm you. And one day, when you were successful, you could come back to your country and rebuild. Your father said, 'the regime cannot take my son's freedom away from me'."

I didn't know what to say. I felt so horrible inside, and my heart sank with regret. I wondered why did I ever leave. Why did I ever put my family in danger? Because of me, now my father is on the front lines, fighting in an unwanted war because there was no choice. What have I done?

I listened carefully as my mother spoke softly in a kind voice and said, "Son, don't worry about us. Try to forget us and make a good life for yourself. Promise me you will continue with your education. Be a good doctor. Maybe one day, we can see each other. May God always be with you. Goodbye." Before I could even respond, the phone went dead. That was the last time that I ever talked to my mother. And then at that moment, I remembered an often-cited quote from a poet master from the thirteenth century named Rumi. He said, "Goodbyes are only for those who love with their eyes. Because for those who love with heart and soul, there is no such thing as separation."

I tried my best to get settled into the United States. Still my thoughts were always on my family that I left behind. I tried on many occasions to contact my family again, but their phone was disconnected. After an exhausting search, it took almost one year to get a number from a neighbor. Finally, I was able to get in contact with them. I vividly remember the conversation. The neighbor said, "Kid, I am very sorry to tell you that your father was killed in the war, and they couldn't even find his body. I am very sorry about the bad news. Unfortunately, when the government official came by your mother's house, they told your mother that your father was killed in action and there was no one to claim his body. When your mother found out, she had a heart attack right there on the spot and passed away. She is with your father in heaven, and I'm sure they are watching over you. You know, they always wanted the best for you. Please forgive us. We couldn't do anything for you. I hope you can forgive us."

I dropped the telephone, dropped to my knees, held my head in my hands and wailed uncontrollably. "My parents are gone" I sobbed. How could I ever live with myself? Why was God punishing me? Is this what it means to be a Christian?

For many years now, I have tried to come to terms with the death of my parents. I often ask myself, *Would things have turned out differently if I had stayed? Or could I have prevented things from happening the way that they did?*

In all honesty, my belief in Christianity was sorely tested during that time. I simply could not understand how a good and righteous God could allow this to happen to me. My parents both sacrificed themselves for my sake so that I could have a better future. Is this what God meant when he said that he sacrificed his son so that mankind could gain everlasting life? Still, whenever I would have bad thoughts like these, Father Fredericks' advice often comes to me: Darius, remember always, stay rooted in faith.

CHAPTER 11

⬦⬦⬦⬦⬦⬦⬦⬦⬦⬦⬦⬦⬦⬦⬦⬦⬦⬦⬦⬦⬦⬦⬦⬦⬦⬦⬦⬦⬦⬦⬦⬦⬦

My Beloved Sandee

(BY DARIUS)

"And in her smile I see something more beautiful
than the stars."

A year later I flew to the West Coast for vacation. I had an aisle
seat on my second flight, and I arrived in my row first. A few minutes later, a beautiful blonde young woman with a medical book in
her hand said, "Excuse me," and I got up to let her into the window
seat. I was relieved that someone who seemed to be near my age was
sitting with me. Nobody else came to our row, and the seat between
us stayed empty. For the final hour of the flight, we spoke nonstop,
learning about each other.

When I first met my wife, Sandee, she was already a doctor. But
I did not know that at the time until I actually got to know her. That
is what attracted me to her. In addition, she is the sweetest person
you could ever meet. She always wants to help others and be best
friends with colleagues.

One day, out of a need for clothing, I decided to go to a nearby
shopping store. It was called Ross. And that was when I first met
Sandee. I remembered seeing her at the University, so when I saw
her again in the store, I felt flustered. I was standing in an aisle, not
knowing exactly where I was, when I noticed that she was nearby.
My hands were full, and somehow I bumped into a rack of cloth-

ing, causing everything to drop loudly to the floor. Feeling embarrassed I started to pick everything up. As I was doing so, a woman approached me and stood over me. When I looked up, it was Sandee. She stood there quietly at first, then she began to laugh. "What are you doing here?" she asked. Then she knelt and began helping me pick up what I had dropped. As she did, she smiled and said, "I knew you were looking at me just now, why didn't you say hi?" Before I could answer, she asked, "Did you know you were in the women's section?" Realizing the truth of her statement, I felt flushed with embarrassment. Not knowing what to do or how to respond, all I could do was stare at her. Sandee then said, "I've noticed you have a strong accent, where are you from?" I quickly responded, "I am from Iran." With that answer, I could see that Sandee was astonished. "Well, since this is our second meeting together, perhaps you can be a gentleman and invite me out for some coffee or tea and then we could talk." I agreed, and as we walked out of the store together, I could sense that Sandee would become very important in my life.

We eventually became best friends and then got married in the church. It was one of the happiest moments of my life. With her love and support, she has helped me to try to forget about the loss of my parents in the unwanted war and other bad situations that I've faced in life.

One year later, God blessed us both with the birth of our beautiful daughter. We named her Artemisia. Then, two years later, God blessed us with yet another daughter, and we named her Farah Claire. So now we are a very happy family. Still the past haunts me, and there is not a day that goes by where I don't think about my parents and their sacrifice.

CHAPTER 12

‹◇◇›

In Memory of Artemisia:
Into the Heavens
(A Warrior for All Time)

"Memories are our greatest inheritance and treasure."

Artemisia was our first daughter and the eldest of our children. Even from an early childhood, she was a tomboy who would always like to get into trouble with other kids. Yet she also was daddy's little girl and the apple of my eye.

Whenever she would ask me, "Dad, what does my name mean?" I would always tell her, your name means, "The great speaker of truth." Then I would go on and explain that it also derives itself from our ancient history. You see, Artemisia was an ancient warrior Princess of Persia. She was the legendary Grand Admiral and leader of the Persian Navy. Also, she was Xerxes' great love. In addition, Artemisia was a great, powerful, independent, and intelligent woman who won many battles during the Achaemenid Dynasty era. So whenever I would tell my daughter about these things, she would always reply to me and say, "I want to be just like her, a warrior princess and help others." Of course, this would always make me smile and laugh with joy. Indeed, Artemisia was very special because she had a way about her that made people happy.

Artemisia was the star and light of our lives. When she finished her college as an athlete, she joined the Virginia State Police Department. I remember that she was so happy when she found out that she got accepted by the department. This was always a dream of hers: to become a state trooper.

Artemisia always would get excited whenever she would talk about the program. She would often tell us about her boot camps and about how she is meeting so many new people and becoming friends with everyone. Artemisia was the type of person who always wanted to help others. She really liked people and wanted to make the city safer for everyone.

After she graduated, she became a really fine state trooper. She was working on highways assisting and helping people involved in car accidents and other calamities. She often received many accolades and awards for the wonderful job that she did around the city.

One day, a coworker needed to get a day off work because she was pregnant and she needed to go to an appointment. So Artemisia, always being a good team player, offered to help her out, even though it would mean that Artemisia would have to do this on her own time. So Artemisia decided to take over the coworker's shift.

It was a very snowy day with blizzardlike conditions outside. On the way to her job, Artemisia could see several vehicles struggle to get through the bad weather, and many had piled up along the side of the road. Blinding snow was coming down hard everywhere and it was extremely difficult to see outside. Artemisia knew that she was going to have a long day ahead of her.

Within minutes upon Artemisia's arrival at work, dispatch radioed, "All available State Troopers, please respond ASAP to several pileups of vehicles on freeway. Use caution." Artemisia responded and told dispatch that she was already on her way.

Artemisia was the first to arrive on the scene. She scanned the area and noticed a vehicle that had overturned. Inside, she could see there was a woman with her two small children. So she rushed to help. She took the two children out of the car first and put them into her police car. Then she went back and retrieved the woman. As they made it safely to her police car, Artemisia radioed for assistance. Realizing that everyone was safe, she decided to put out some roadside flares near the accident to let other drivers be on the alert. Unfortunately, while making her way back to her patrol vehicle, she was struck by a truck which lost control in the blinding snow and hit Artemisia. The rescued woman and her two children had to watch in horror as Artemisia was dragged several hundred yards. When the ambulance arrived, instead of attending to the woman and her two children, they immediately tried to help pry out Artemisia's mangled body from the wreckage. Artemisia suffered severe brain damage and head trauma along with multiple broken bones. Ten days later, she passed away. It was a terrible loss and tragedy for everyone involved, especially her family.

I remembered how at the funeral the Virginia Governor and the Chief of State Police spoke about Artemisia. They said that she was highly motivated, always willing to help others, and a kind person. They called her one of the city's greatest heroes and how the State's Police Department had lost one of its best. It seemed as if half of the city was mourning for her on that day.

My family and I could not believe that Artemisia was so loved by so many of her colleagues and friends.

After the governor gave the last speech, a 21-gun salute was heard and then Taps was played. As Taps played, the Chief of the State police came over and presented Sandee with the American flag. Sandee couldn't help herself anymore; her emotions got the best of her, and she sobbed as the flag was placed into her hands. Several minutes later, Artemisia was carried off to her final resting place. With tears streaming down my eyes as we both gazed over the huge crowd of attendees, all that I could say to my wife was, "God is great."

CHAPTER 13

<><><><><><><><><><><><><><><><><><><><><><><><><><><><><><><><><><><><><><>

When Faith Is Shaken

"Faith isn't believing without proof—it's trusting without reservation."

Sometimes, I ask God why this is happening to us. And I often beg him to please help us, please bring back my beloved child. I don't want anything else but to just have my family back, please if you can. Unfortunately, there is nothing anyone can do except mourn the loss. So we cried for many days afterward.

After several months of sadness and mourning, I could not go to work. My colleagues were getting worried about me. Then, one day I got a call from the hospital. Apparently, they needed my assistance quickly because there was a patient who needed heart surgery right away. So I rushed to the hospital and offered help.

After a while, my wife and I got enough strength and began to talk about the death of our beloved daughter, Artemisia. It was painful at first, but we needed to do this so that we could have some healing. And it was a huge challenge for us because we felt that we needed a miracle to bring us back to a sense of normal and to make us a family again. Artemisia's death was a catalyst for change.

I picked up my Bible and began to read it. This was the very same Bible that Father Fredericks had given to me when he was back in Tehran. Somehow, I flipped to a chapter and began to read.

My family and I also received hundreds of letters from sympathetic people around the country. For several weeks, people from the media wanted my family and I to share their story. But out of respect for the family, I decided not to go forward on this at the time. Sometimes I would read some of the letters to Sandee and Farah. One particular letter was especially touching because it was from someone in the White House. It read:

> As life goes on, days rolling into nights, it will become clear that you never really stop missing someone special who's gone. You just learn to live around the gaping hole of their absence. When you lose someone that you can't imagine living without, your heart breaks wide open. And the bad news is that you never completely get over the loss because you will never forget them. However, in a backward way, this is also the good news. You see, they will live on in the warmth of your broken heart that doesn't fully heal back up. And you will continue to grow and experience life, even with your wound. It's like breaking an ankle that never heals perfectly. And that still hurts you when you dance. But you dance anyway but with a slight limp. And this limps just adds to the depth of your performance and the authenticity of your character. The people you lose remain a part of you. Remember them and always cherish the good memories spent with them.

I loved this letter so much that I had it framed and kept it on the in a prominent position. Of course, I still carried the note from Father Fredericks. Often, I would pull out the crumpled note and read it: Darius, remember, always stay rooted in faith.

CHAPTER 14

◇✕✕✕✕✕✕✕✕✕✕✕✕✕✕✕✕✕✕✕✕✕✕✕◇

Farah Claire: Journey into the Unknown

"If no one ever told you, your freedom is more important than their anger."

Farah Claire is our second daughter. She is also the younger sister of Artemisia, who died in a terrible car accident. Of course, it has been very hard for Farah Claire to cope with the loss, especially her parents. Yet despite the loss and the pain, Farah Claire came to realize that she had to be strong for everyone.

Several years after, Farah Claire finished high school. She decided to go to medical school at Virginia State University. Her motivation was simple: she did this as a way of honoring her big sister, Artemisia. Farah Claire always looked up to her. In her eyes and heart, Artemisia was her hero and best friend who always pushed her to be better and always help out.

I remember the first day of school at the University when we dropped her off. There were many people, and everyone was happy. Some people were crying; others were laughing before they said goodbye to their families. When it came time for Farah Claire to go, she proudly stood beside us and asked us for our permission, which is custom. I remember looking deeply into her eyes and telling her, "Farah, you are ready, so go get it!"

Well, I'm in the United States, in the beautiful state of Virginia. And after two years I took the enrollment tests and enrolled in the University of Virginia state. I did this for myself and my family because I promised them that I would continue with my education goals. Also, I want to be a good doctor. It has taken me over ten years now, but I've become a junior heart surgeon.

Still, I wish my family was with me. It pains me immensely when I realize that both of my parents are gone and they cannot share in my success. At times, I often feel guilty because of the sacrifices that they made for me. Yet, I also realize that somehow life must go on—even when it seems that you cannot. I know and believe that God, in his infinite wisdom, has a purpose and a destiny for all of his children.

CHAPTER 15

Farah Claire: A New Beginning at Life

"Let go of yesterday. Let today be a new beginning and be the best that you can, and you'll get
to where God wants you to be."

I cannot believe it, but it is happening. I am already in the University. It feels so unbelievable, but it's real. I'm here ready to open another chapter of my life. After I introduced myself to my classmates and the dean, we were guided to the dormitory. The next day I was introduced to the teachers, the library, and other staff. I really liked the peaceful environment, and there were so many people from other continents, especially Asia and Africa. On the weekends, they would have their own festivals or cultural exchanges.

The first and second month went by quickly, and I made many friends. We were so fascinated by each other's cultures. There was a lot of studying that went on. I got to know many of the teachers. There were always so many questions about human physiology and sickness and how ancient doctors could cure their people with simple and basic natural ingredients. It was mind-boggling to see how far human beings have come in medicine.

CHAPTER 16

<><><><><><><><><><><><><><><><><><><><><><><><><><><><><><><><><><><><><><><>

Steve, the Love of My Life

(by Farah Claire)

"As long as I have a heartbeat, I'm fine. So I just
do what I love and I do it the best that I can. And
if it all goes away, I'll just start over."

About eight months into the classes, I had the opportunity to
meet a colleague. His name was Steve, and he was a captain in the
United States Marines Corps who had already been deployed several
times to Iraq and Afghanistan. I met him at the University during
lunchtime. He was handsome, tall, blonde haired, and with piercing
blue eyes; and I was immediately attracted to him from the start. To
my surprise, I heard this very strong voice come up to me. He asked
me in a kind and caring voice if it was okay to sit next to me because
there was no seat available. I smiled and meekly replied and said yes,
feeling awkward at the time. As I looked around, I could hear and
see that many of the other women in the area were now staring at us.
This would become the beginning of a friendship that would later
blossom into something much deeper.

It was during the second week of our knowing each other that
Steve asked me out for a date. Of course, I was so surprised and
a bit alarmed because things were moving along pretty fast for the
both of us. I didn't know what to say. So I called my parents and ask
them for their permission. This was becoming my very first serious

relationship, and I just didn't know what to do. Of course, my parents encouraged me to embrace the relationship. However, they also warned me to be careful and take things slowly. With their love and support, I decided to give it a try.

Steve and I talked about everything from politics, to medicine, to movies, and more. It seemed as if we shared the same thoughts and ideas. This always amazed me and brought me much joy. On one occasion, Steve asked me why I had not considered joining the military. I told him that I wanted to serve my country but wasn't sure. Later on, after I realized my talents, I changed my mind. And with Steve's encouragement, I enlisted in the military. It was a really big deal for me because of all the uncertainty. Still, I felt that I had made a good decision because it was my dream.

I think that mostly I wanted to help others while I served my country. So after several days, I asked my dad if it would be okay to join the Navy as a medical personnel to serve my country. He said, "Let me talk to your mom, I'll let you know." I was happy and scared at the same time as I didn't know how my parents would react to this. Well, after a couple of weeks, I got their blessing, and I enlisted two months later. I joined the Navy, it was fun, and it felt like something I was born to do. After boot camps and training, I joined the medical field. I continued my education until graduation.

One day, as we were talking at lunch at the University, Steve's phone began ringing. He realized right away that it was an international call, so he quickly excused himself to answer it. He went a few feet away, but I could still hear the conversation. The caller was talking in what sounded like a distressed voice, with broken English. They sounded like they were from Afghanistan. The person wanted to ask for help but was unable to convey the message. Steve could not understand what the person on the other line was saying. I recognized the language and asked if I could help translate. Steve looked surprised and couldn't say anything. He handed me the phone as an answer. I began speaking and writing the request. The caller's name was Mohammad Sharif from Kabul, Afghanistan. He was Steve's interpreter. He was calling to ask Steve's permission to become a sponsor, so he could obtain a green visa because he is eligible. The work he did with the U.S. forces made him eligible for the green card visa through the military. Steve, and everyone around us had their mouths opened in shock. I was talking so fast and taking notes at the same time whike translating what was being said. It was second nature to me because of my father. I would often help him volunteer with refugees from Iraq and Afghanistan for medical and transportation needs. My father always taught me to take notes while translating. Steve was shocked, happy, and a little bit bewildered. "How can you do all that at one time?" he asked. "Do you realize how valuable your skills would be in other parts of the world? I wish I had you on my team when I was deployed to Iraq and Afghanistan. Many times, we have serious difficulties in translations between our local and U.S. linguists due to nuances in the American language. Also, a lot of military acronyms and terms which are critical cannot be understood by other cultures." I wondered if he was right. I never thought about joining the U.S. Navy. With Steve's encouragement, I decided to enlist and become a Naval Medical Officer and serve my country. I knew I would be making a commitment and sacrifice, but I was determined to follow my dreams and see what Steve had experienced. I could use the military to further my education, get my degree so I could become a medical doctor, and travel around the globe utilizing my skills to help others in need. So that is exactly what I did."

I replied, "Wow, I did not know that you served in the US military. I'm surprised to learn that about you. So not only are you handsome, but you're also a war hero too? By the way, thank you for your service. I think that many people don't appreciate the sacrifices military individuals make to keep our country safe. Steve smiled and said it is my honor and duty to serve my country."

Over the course of the next several months, I developed a wonderful friendship with Steve that would later blossom into a beautiful relationship. Steve explained how he came to enlist in the military. His intriguing story made me laugh, cry, and wonder. *Could it be possible for someone to be that selfless?* I wondered.

Steve told me about the hardships of people in other parts of the world, due to his many encounters with those in civilizations such as Afghanistan and Iraq. Many people suffered and struggled for basic necessities, such as food, water, medical needs, and shelter. Many service men had never been in a situation in which they were not prepared to face.

Realizing this was a problem, Steve contacted his hometown and requested for help. Operation Care Package came to the rescue. These Care Packages were sent from home to servicemen deployed overseas. Steve received a Care Package from the States. It was packed with all the essentials that a person needed like food stuffs, personal hygiene items, and more. So he decided to share his package with some of the locals. This turned out to be very successful. Whenever a Care Package was given out to the locals, a picture was taken of the recipients. This became a huge winning point for Steve and his unit and really help to motivate and establish good relations with the local Afghanis. It also prevented future attacks against his unit because it fostered a sense of friendship with the locals. Steve was always amazed at how just a little kindness could go a long way.

I almost forgot about this: Several months later, Steve and I become a couple, and now we live together. I remember it like it was yesterday. Steve made it a very special day for everyone. He wanted us to be married in our military uniforms, which we did. And he wanted the celebration to be on base at the Officers Club. It was a big affair, and he invited all of his colleagues. There were a total of about 150 people that attended, including Steve's commander and many of his fellow officers. There was dancing, good food, music; and it was a very beautiful affair. Of course, during the celebration, Steve got down on bended knee and proposed to me. I was totally unprepared for this, but of course I said yes. So now we are married, and I couldn't be any happier.

We've been together now for over two years. And in that time, Steve has been promoted to the rank of Major, and now I'm a Junior Medical officer. My family is so proud of me. I just wish that my big sister was here to see me, especially in my uniform. I always remember her. But it's okay because I know she is always with us.

While being a Junior Medical Doctor had its ups and downs, it does have its advantages. Firstly, we get the opportunity to travel to many faraway places around the world. For example, with the U.S. Navy, I did get to travel to South America and Asia. In the Philippines when there was a disaster and people need lots of help, the U.S. Navy dispatched us. I can see people needed basic medical and surviving materials, so we tried to provide all the help we could. It felt good to know the U.S. Navy and U.S. aid was there to help others. I am so proud of my country. After my tour of duty from Asia, I continued my study and I learned more about medical fields by volunteering in emergency rooms, shelters, and even jails.

When Steve came back from his latest mission in Afghanistan, I got a letter from the US Navy. It said that I was going to deploy to Afghanistan for one year. Of course, my family was very worried because they could see on the television all the terrible news about the war in Afghanistan and the horrible situation about Taliban-Al Qaeda and others. However, I felt that it was my duty, and I have to do it. When I discuss it with my husband, Steve asked me, "Are you sure that you want to do this?" I told him the truth and said no, which is how I actually felt. But I also explained to him that I felt I had an obligation to go because I made a commitment to the military. In addition, since I'm going there as a medical officer, they could use my skills. I jokingly said to him, "What can possibly go wrong?" Little did I know what was about to come for me in the days and weeks ahead and how dramatically my life would change.

The following month I said goodbye to my husband, Steve, and my family and headed for Afghanistan. It was very difficult to leave my husband and my family behind, but I had made a commitment and I wanted to help out.

Steve told me a lot of things about Afghanistan, both good and bad. He said that during his deployment there, he ran into a lot of corrupted officials. However, he said that he also got to meet many good people of Afghanistan. Many people just simply wanted to leave and have a better life for themselves and their children, but they were caught in the war either as refuges or casualties.

When we landed in Kuwait, the weather was very hot. A sand-storm greeted us upon our arrival, and you could not see anything in front of you. We had to get to the shelter as soon as possible until the weather subsided.

Now we are at Kuwait Air Force Base with many NATO and allied soldiers from all forty nations. It is so beautiful when you can hear every dialect and every accent you can think of, especially when we go to eat at the military dining facility.

Immediately, we became friends with so many doctors and nurses from different countries. They were going on the same mission as us, some go to Iraq and some to Afghanistan. We were worried but also excited to see the country at war. We didn't know what to expect when we got there. Finally, the Captain and head of our medical team came out. "Next week we are going to Afghanistan. Please contact your families and let them know you are going to a war zone. After we had the captain's meeting, we all went to a nearby phone and Internet café to contact our families and let them know we were leaving.

I spoke to Steve via Skype on the computer. We talked for more than an hour, and I told him everything. We both laughed and cried, and he wished me luck on my mission to Afghanistan. Little did I know what was in store for me. However, I think that he knew that I would be going into a combat zone, but he wanted to reassure me to stay strong and always be prepared.

CHAPTER 17

<><><><><><><><><><><><><><><><><><><><><><><><><><><><><><><><><><><><><><><><>

In Search of Father Fredericks

"Life is full of happiness and tears; be strong and
have faith."

Despite my hectic schedule with school classes, there is one
thing that always bothered me, I often wondered, *Why can't I find
Father Fredericks?* But after a couple of years and a lot of research
and contacts with missionaries around the United States, I finally
was able to locate Matthew who is the son of Father Fredericks. It
was such a joy! Unfortunately, Matthew didn't remember me. So I
explained who I was.

After I explained myself, Matthew told me that he and his
mother, along with James and Father Fredericks, were doing some
missionary work in Ghana, West Africa. Matthew said that once they
all finished with the missionary work there, they would contact me.

I felt very happy. All that I kept thinking was I finally located
the man who is responsible for putting me on my journey to joy,
happiness, and freedom. My thoughts went back to the time when
Father Fredericks first introduced me to the Bible and the words of
Jesus Christ. "Do you accept Jesus Christ as your Lord and Savior?
Do you accept Christianity and all that it teaches?" Yes, I do," I said.
And from that moment on, I've tried to be a good Christian. It has
not always been easy; in fact, at times it's been really difficult. Father

Fredericks gave me hope, he said "Darius, always remember to stay rooted in faith."

Then one day, Matthew contacted me and told me that he had found his father's phone number. I was so elated that for two days I debated within myself as to what I should say to him. I was so excited that I just didn't know how to talk to the man who was responsible for my happiness. Finally, I got the courage to call him.

What a day! He remembered me. I could not believe it. I started crying and telling him about all that as happening in my country and with my family. We both laughed and cried so many times, but I was happy at last. He promised me to come visit me so as soon as he was done in his mission in Africa. I can't wait to introduce Father Frederick's to my family. I'm sure they're going to be very happy because I always told them about my experience and how I got through all my difficulty when I was younger, especially with the war. Father Fredericks and his words of wisdom gave me strength to make it.

CHAPTER 18

<><><><><><><><><><><><><><><><><><><><><><><><><><><><><><><><><><><><><><><><><><><><><>

In Memory of Bella

"Remember that shadow is temporary. Love and
Light are the truer and stronger reality."

Sometimes whenever I hear a dog bark from a distance, it
makes me automatically remember our beloved dog Bella. She was
a beautiful German shepherd that was given to me by one of Dad's
heart-transplant patients. He was from Germany, and then he sent
Bella from Germany to us as a gift. It was a token of his appreciation
for helping him with the surgery. At that time, Bella was one-year-
old, but we quickly learned that she was very smart. Bella learned
to interact with patients and was especially good at interacting with
children. We would often take Bella to the hospital because he was
always eager to help. Sometimes we would take Bella and listen to his
heart with a stethoscope. It was always amazing to hear how strong
Bella's heartbeat was.

Everything changed for the worse when on one sad day some
neighborhood kids were running around in the street. A kid named
Tommy always liked to play with Bella. So we let Tommy play with
Bella. While we were talking, one of the kids throw a ball into the
street. Tommy ran after it, right into an incoming car. However, Bella
was able to sense what was going on, and before the car was about to
strike the kid, Bella ran and jumped in front of the vehicle and was
hit by the vehicle. Bella took the brunt force of the hit and saved the

kid's life. Unfortunately, Bella died several days later from internal injuries as a result of the accident. For many weeks and months afterward, I was sad and depressed, and I still cry to this very day when I think of Bella. Still, the pleasant memories that Bella left behind always warm my heart. It is true, a dog is definitely a man's best friend. We will always love you, Bella!

CHAPTER 19

<><><><><><><><><><><><><><><><><><><><><><><><><><><><><><><><><><><>

Welcome to Helmand Province
of Afghanistan (Part 1)

"Be fearless in the pursuit of what sets your soul
on fire."

Helmand Province is one of the thirty-four provinces of
Afghanistan, in the south of the country. It is the largest province by
area, covering 58,584 square kilometers (20,000 square miles) area.
The province contains thirteen districts, encompassing over 1,000
villages, and roughly 879,500 settled people. Lashkar Gah serves as
the provincial capital.

The Helmand province campaign was a series of military operations conducted by the International Security Assistance Force
(ISAF) forces against Taliban insurgents in the Helmand Province
of Afghanistan. Their objective was to control a province that was
known to be a Taliban stronghold, and a center of opium production.

The deployment of international, mostly British, forces was
part of the stage three expansion of the ISAF mandate, to cover the
southern regions of Afghanistan. Until then, Helmand province had
seen only a limited coalition presence.

In the spring of 2008, a battalion of US Marines arrived to
reinforce the British presence. In the spring of 2009, 11,000 addi-

tional Marines poured into the province, the first wave of President Obama's 21,000-troop surge into Afghanistan.

On June 19, 2009, the British Army (with ISAF and ANA forces) launched Operation Panther's Claw, and on July 2, 2009, the US Marines launched Operation Khanjar, both major offensives into the province in hopes of securing the region before the Afghanistan presidential elections and turning the tide of the insurgency there.

Two days later, we arrived at Kuwait airport and had a two-day layover. Afterward, we boarded a C-17 aircraft, and after several hours, we made it to Bagram Air Force in Afghanistan.

Once we got there, nearby at the checkpoint gate, there was a lot of people protesting against U.S. forces. We didn't know why they are there for. So I asked one of the soldiers why are people protesting, and he told me because there was a man on the United States tour in the part of the holy book of Muslims Qur'an (the Qur'an is the holy book for Muslims, revealed in stages to the Prophet Muhammad over twenty-three years). Quranic revelations are regarded by Muslims as the sacred word of God, intended to correct any errors in previous holy books (such as the Old and New Testaments). After several hours, with the help of US Marines and Afghan soldiers and police, people left the base and dispersed. God, I was getting nervous because I never saw so many people at the ministry gate chanting death to the United States. It was a really very bad experience.

My first duty station was at the Bagram Air Force Hospital. While I was there, I learned a lot about triage emergencies and how to deal with injured Soldiers, Marines, Airmen, and Sailors. We have to work ten-hour shifts every day, but I met a lot of other doctors and nurses on the emergency situation. We also have lots of locals coming for medical needs and help, and one of the biggest problems was the lack of medicine for local Afghans. Our mission was to treat everybody the same. So we take care of everybody as soon as they arrived to the emergency room.

Since my dad was originally from Iran, he taught me how to speak Farsi and Dari. These are two separate languages that are spoken in Afghanistan. It always amazes many people of Afghanistan when they see me and learn that I speak their language. Of course, they are all shocked and surprised. They can't help but wonder how an American with blonde hair and green eyes is able to speak our language. I have to always explain my dad's origin of coming from Iran, then it makes sense to people.

I have many good memories from Iran. Many Iranians are very friendly people. I also have good memory because we are immigrants in that country.

I find lots of friends among local Afghani women and children. I can talk to them, connect with them, listen to their stories, laugh with them, and cry with them. When I received a lot of gifts from my family and friends, I give them to the local children and their families. I tried to share happiness with them. So many times when the patient arrived, they asked for me by name. They would say, "I want to see Dr. Farah please. Is she here?" So, I was happy to help even when I was asleep or when I was off, my colleagues would call, "Dr. Farah, you have to come here. We have locals looking for you, saying you are the only they want to help them." I would laugh and go there to help assist in what they needed and remind them that the other doctors were there to help them too. I encouraged them to continue their education, but sometimes it was hard because they were afraid to be persecuted by the men in their familiesUnder the Taliban regime, it was illegal for women to go to school or University. Imagine that.

After several months, the US general in charge of the hospital, General Atkinson, called me to his office. After a small ceremony, he presented me with a certificate along with a coin and congratulated me for all the hard work that I was accomplishing. Then he took me aside and told me privately, "We have a very special mission for you. However, it is dangerous and you will be in an open outpost. It is located in Helmand Province. We have chosen you because of your background, which is linguistics and medical. Even though we hate to lose you here, your skills are in more need there. I believe that you can really make a difference there. Also, if you do well there, your chances of being promoted will increase. So I'd like you to think about it and give me your answer not later than tomorrow."

Of course, I accepted the mission. I felt that I really had an obligation and a duty to help out, which is what my big sister would have done also. So I went to the MWR (Military, Welfare, and Recreation) and contacted Steve via Skype.

I explained to Steve what was going on. At first he laughed and said, "Are you serious?" Then when he realized that I was telling the truth, he said, "Okay, well, since you are going, let me share some things that I know. You will need to prepare yourself because Helmand Province is the most dangerous place in all of Afghanistan. You will need to always be on guard and be prepared for anything, especially ambushes, which occur in that province frequently. Helmand Province is also one of the main centers for the opium trade and hometown of the Taliban. So please always be extra vigilant. I love you always, and I will pass on to the family that you will be going into a combat zone so that we can pray for your safe return. God bless." So with Steve's blessing, I ended the Skype connection and proceeded to prepare for deployment.

CHAPTER 20

<<<<<<<<<<<<<<<<<<<<<<<<<<<<<<<<<<<<<<<<<<<<<<<<<<<<<<<

Welcome to Helmand Province of Afghanistan (Part 2)

"No matter how dark it might get, hope and faith will always light the way."

The following week, I was at the airport taking a helicopter ride. Our first stop was Kandahar, Afghanistan. After that, we traveled to Helmand Province.

We were a team of eight people, including two doctors and six Navy Corpsman. Once we landed, we traveled in a military convoy to Lashkar Gah, which is a very small city in southern Afghanistan and the capital of Helmand Province.

Well, it was chaos. As soon as we landed, the Taliban fighters started shooting some mortars and RPGs (Rocket Propelled Grenades) at the base. So we all had to run to safety, a safety zone located at the nearby bunker. After about thirty minutes, there was a cease-fire heard through the base intercom system telling everyone it was safe to come out. Wow! What a rush; I didn't know what to do about this type of situation because I'd never done anything like this before. However, it was just like Steve told me, you have to be ready for anything.

We were working very hard to fulfill all of the medical needs of the local people. There were so many people coming up to the checkpoint on a daily basis asking for help. Some people needed assistance for grants to rebuild their houses and shops due to damage incurred during the firefight between coalition forces and Taliban fighters. And others simply were suffering from diarrhea and many other diseases and were in desperate need of medical assistance. Others were pregnant and needed help with basic prenatal care. We tried to do our best. However, there were instances where we could do nothing.

For example, we have older men (Mullahs) who would often forcefully choose a younger-aged bride from age nine to fourteen years. In many instances, the bride would be related to someone close to the mullah. (A *mullah* is a term of respect used to describe an educated religious man). However, the majority of time, none of them could read or write. They were simply given the name by their forefathers). Of course, this created a huge problem because many children would be born mentally challenged and unstable, almost retarded. Many would later develop Down syndrome, and they were often called Monguls. The saddest part of this tragedy is that many of the children would often be sold at the lowest price to wealthy older men. Sometimes the child-bride would be suicidal or would try to run away once they learned the truth about themselves. Whenever I encountered these types of situations, I would always cry and become very sad. Because the child-bride would tell me that they had been raped or abused. I tried to cope with the situation, but it was extremely difficult. Ironically, whenever I discussed it with my chain of command, I was always told the same thing: it's not our business to interfere with Afghan laws. I could not understand how we could just go along with this policy, just walk away and close our eyes about this matter. So it bothered me all the time.

In the meantime, I was treating all of my patients. Also, because of my linguistic skills, I was interpreting local Afghan to my nurses. It was important because they needed to know about what medicine they needed and what problems they have and how best can we can help them. Of course, everybody was extremely surprised at how I could multitask every day. For me, the credit goes to my father, who taught me how to do this, and I'm grateful for his teachers.

Two months soon passed by very quickly. Then, Capt. Jonathan, the head of the medical team at Helmand Province, came to me and asked me for another favor. He said he had another mission. He told me that I was a great asset and that he had heard a lot of good things about me and my work. "However, we have a severe need for your services in a place near the Pakistan border called Garshmir District. It is located in the southern part of Helmand Province, Afghanistan, with many villages along the Helmand River. They are in desperate need of medical assistance, doctors, Navy Corpsman, and nurses.

"In that area, we have another small outpost with several villages along the Helmand River with the opium fields. Currently, we do not have enough assets to build any clinic; however, we will do so in the near future. In the meantime, we need your help. Would you be interested to go there for two weeks and then come back?" he asked me politely.

Of course, I said yes, I would be honored to go and work in that area and fulfill any needs. And so the mission began.

CHAPTER 21

<><><><><><><><><><><><><><><><><><><><><><><><><><><><><><><><><><><><><><><>

Taken: Prisoner of War (POW)

"Once we know of atrocities, we cannot remain
silent, and knowledge inevitably leads to an urge
to protect the innocent."

I was part of a military convoy of sixty, which include Humvees, five-ton trucks, Multirole Armored Vehicles (MRAVs), Armored SUVs, and Armored Personnel Carriers (APCs). The mission was to drop me off at the small outpost along with several US Marines, medical, and food supplies. Unfortunately, after several hours into the route, the front scout vehicle hit an IED (Improvised Explosive Device), and the driver and gunner were badly wounded. Immediately, the entire convoy had to stop, and my vehicle had to go to the front. After the Marine bomb detection team disarmed the other IEDs, they brought the two wounded Marines back to a safe area. I attended to the wounded soldiers. I immediately went to work remembering my training in the triage. I applied tourniquets on the arms and legs of the injured Marines and bandaged their wounds. Both marines were hit with several shrapnel (bomb fragments that cause horrific injuries and can include nails, metal shards, and ball bearings). This made it very difficult to perform any operations. So I contacted the Captain and requested a Medevac (Medical Evacuation Helicopter). About thirty minutes later, the Medevac arrived. A safe area was highlighted with chem lights and colored-smoke grenade, which identified the landing zone. In the meantime, several vehicles and Humvees posted a 360-degree circle to protect the landing zone from any further attacks. Of course, everyone was worried about the safety of the two injured Marines and what if the helicopter landed, would the Taliban fighters be waiting and launch another RPG attack? Then, in the distance, I could see and hear three Black Hawk helicopters approaching. One was identified with a Red Cross (US Army Medevac). The other two were escorts with machine guns ready for any attacks from the ground.

The sight of wounded Marines stunned me. I realized that I was in shock and disbelief because although I had been trained, nothing could prepare me for this. Yet my training kicked in, and both Marines were evacuated successfully.

Now it was already dark, and everyone had to use their night-vision goggles because we were not allowed to turn vehicle headlights on. This would alert the enemy that we were in the area, and it would allow them to be able to shoot the vehicles with an RPG or roadside bomb or small arms fire.

As soon as I made it safely to the outpost, the rest of the convoy said goodbye and continued to another destination for a resupply.

I was surprised but relieved that we made it to the outpost Bravo safely. I was introduced to the rest of the US Marines and briefed on their mission. As soon as I was being guided to my tent, a firefight started between the Taliban and the US Marines at the post. The firefight was so intense that it lasted several hours, and the US Marines dispatched air support from the nearby US Air Base in Qandahar. Then about thirty minutes later, two US Apache helicopters arrived and began to fire at the enemy positions. They were able to kill at least fifteen Taliban and injured many others. In the end, the enemy was forced to run away. Thank God, I thought to herself. I was so scared and didn't know what to expect because so many bullets and RPGs were flying overhead; some managed to strike the walls of the small compound. It was a very scary night for everyone.

Afterward, in the early morning hours, everyone helped to repair sandbags and fix the defensive walls. It had to be done every day in order to ensure that everyone was safe from enemy fire.

The next day, everything was nice and quiet. All you could hear is the sound of livestock nearby. The scenery stood in stark contrast to what had occurred on the previous night. The outpost was located next to the Helmand River. Also, there were lots of opium fields, fruit gardens, and open green land that were filled with many livestock, such as sheep, goats, donkeys, and cows, which would often graze upon the land. Often we had to take showers in the river. This is due to the fact that we did not have any shower or restrooms in the outpost. On many occasions while we were taking showers in the river, we had to be escorted by two marines along with many local children who would watch us in fascination. Often they would ask us for our soap or shampoo because it smelled good. Near the post, the local children felt safe to interact with the U.S. Marines and me. The majority of the younger children became friends. In fact, they seemed fascinated with my hair color because it was unusual to have a blonde female Marine in the area with no scarf. In addition, they often would ask me if it was all right to touch my hair. Of course, I said it was okay, and when they did touch it, they would laugh and smile and say it's so soft. It smelled so good. Surprisingly, they learned some American words, such as hello, thank you, give me, etc.

My mornings usually started with me greeting all of the local Afghan patients at the gate. Because they did not have an interpreter at the time, I had to do everything by myself. The US Marines Lieutenant was very surprised to see that I could speak the language. Also, the local Afghans were amazed that I could speak their language too. After a while, I became so good at it that I even learned their slang and accents from the local Afghans. Oftentimes, I would laugh and cry with them because I understood.

So I became famous and popular at the same time. Because of my uniqueness, a blonde female, soldier in their area, lots and lots of people were coming to see me. Somehow, word spread about me to the Taliban fighters and their commander. Unfortunately, this turned out to be disadvantageous because it led to more attacks against the outpost.

In the meantime, the local villages kept coming to visit me. Some had serious medical problems; other basically just wanted to see the U.S. female doctor who could speak their language. Sometimes things were very funny and unusual for me. For example, if I gave one person ibuprofen for pain relief, as soon as the first person would come out and tell the others what I gave him/her, everybody else would ask for ibuprofen. Ibuprofen is red in color, and everybody loves that color.

Then, one night there was an incident which occurred at about 8:00 PM. There was a woman in the distance who looked like she was pregnant. She was having difficulty walking and was screaming for help. Along with her there appeared to be her mother and a small child, a boy. The Marines had a checkpoint and had to stop these villagers. So they radioed the Lieutenant about the situation. They said, "We have two females and a boy approaching us. It looks like one of the females is pregnant and in need of medical attention. They are shouting at us and we don't understand." So the lieutenant then rushed to my tent, woke me up, and explained the situation. I was asked to come assess the situation and provide assistance because no one could speak the language except me and they did not have available interpreters. Also, due to the dangerous area, no local interpreters were willing to work with the US Marines at the time. If they did, they feared retaliation on their families. Of course, this made the situation even worse.

I rushed to the checkpoint and assess the situation. The Marines shouted at the pregnant woman and the child, "Put your hands up!" I immediately translated the request. All the villagers then put their hands up. The Marines silently uttered to me, "We must check them for weapons and suicide vests." So, the two Marines and I approached the villagers cautiously. I began to search for possible weapons. Once it was clear, I began to assist the villagers. That was when I noticed the woman was pregnant but in great pain. So, I told to the Marines "We must get the pregnant woman into the compound because she is in severe pain and I need to give her medication. We also might need to have her Medevac'd." As soon as I started to help the patient, there was a barrage of gunfire. It came from the front and from the sides. Immediately, everyone took cover.

I grabbed the pregnant woman and ducked behind a small tree with bushes. The two Marines ducked out of sight behind a large Boulder and began to return fire from the location of the firefight. Unfortunately, I was separated from the two Marines. The lieutenant yelled at me to come back, that the two Marines would cover me. But it was no use because it was chaos. I was confused and more worried about the safety of the pregnant woman than myself. In the end, I hid and sheltered the pregnant woman behind the tree.

In all the confusion, the two Marines left the safety of the Boulder, and rushed back to the compound, thinking that I was following behind them. When they reach to the compound, the Lieutenant asked where I was. To their shock and disbelief, they didn't have an answer. They thought I was right behind them.

I stayed clumped together shielding the pregnant women and the one child. I froze and began to pray for all of their safety. Unfortunately, the Taliban fighters began to mobilize once they saw the two marines had treated. This emboldened them, and they began to intensify the firefight. They launched more RPGs against the outpost and at the same time they surrounded me and began yelling. Due to the commotion, I was hit with a bullet to the ankle and fell down in pain. The bullet passed through my military boots into the sand, leaving a gaping hole. At that moment, I looked up to see myself being surrounded by several Taliban fighters. In the meantime, I was still shielding the pregnant woman and the small boy. "Where are the marines at?" I wondered. But it was too late.

One man grabbed my ankles, one in each hand, and dragged me out away from the cover of the tree and out into the open. I screamed out in agony. My instinct was to struggle a bit, not wanting the indignity of being dragged from my shelter against my will, but the violent jerk on my wounded ankle made me scream out in pain. To my disbelief, the pregnant woman and the mother along with the son came to my rescue and began pleading for my release. The Taliban fighters retaliated in the worse way by pointing their weapons at the villagers and saying, "If you don't go back, we will kill you." However, the pregnant female picked up a small stone and threw it at one of the Taliban fighters. That angers all of the other Taliban fighters. So they all started shooting the two innocent females along with the small child. I screamed out in horror as I watched helplessly while all three Afghans were killed right in front of my eyes. They showed absolutely no remorse, no feelings—just sadistic cold-blooded murder.

Agony washed up my legs and exploded through me. Now putting up a fight dimmed to nothing after that. I realized I was helpless.

Boots, sandaled feet, and weapon butts came out from everywhere, hitting my arms, my head, and my wounded ankle. I cowered and covered up, trying to protect my head and body, but the kicks and the triumphant shouts of the angry men around me went on and on.

I had no idea how many of them were there. We had killed some of them. They had killed some of us, and they were the victors. They were all yelling at once, but I understood every word of it. They were furious, yelling, "Death to Satan, death to America." They were wild with victory; they were really hurting me, and I wasn't convinced that they weren't done killing people. I thought they might literally tear me apart in their frenzy.

The pummeling continued for a long time. Finally, one major kick connected squarely at my head, knocking my helmet off, and the body armor went rolling away. The man who kicked my helmet started talking excitedly, pushing and shoving others out of the way. As I lay there for a second, expecting more blows to come at any time, he violently pulled the rest of my gear off along with the medical backpack. There was a long pause as they stared down at me, and I realized they were figuring out that I was a woman. They confirmed her sex with a violent check to see if I had breasts. They all seemed to be enjoying the search of my body parts as they molested me repeatedly. There was more excited talking, pushing, and shoving around me; but evidently having boobs meant the beatings would stop. There wasn't time to take much comfort in that.

Out of nowhere, two Taliban fighters grabbed me up, and the other one hit me in the head with the butt of his gun. I passed out from the blow, and they dragged me away into the darkness.

A day and a half later, I woke up and found myself tied up and chained to a heavy large black anvil in a small dark room. It looked like it was used for livestock. The smell of animal urine and feces mixed with haze was all around.

After a while, the door suddenly opened, and sunlight came into the room, causing me to squint my eyes. At that moment, I noticed a woman with a very distinctive accent saying something, but I could not understand what the woman was saying because I was still dazed. The woman came over to me and showed me some Afghan female clothing along with Afghan traditional cover (*burqa*). She placed the clothing next to me and quickly left the room. Then I passed out again.

When I awoke, I saw myself clothed in Afghan clothing. My wounds had been attended to with basic rags that were poorly adjusted. My uniform was nearby, but it had blood on it. So I began to clean my wounds and fix myself up with new antiseptic from the medical bag. I also gave myself some shots to prevent infection because I realized the bullet has passed through my ankle. Finally, I stitched herself up. It was very painful because I did not have the appropriate tools, but I managed.

While I was looking at the medical bag, I noticed a picture tucked down on the bottom of the bag. I took it out and looked at it closely. I soon realized it was a picture of me and my husband, Steve, along with the entire family on our wedding day. I gently kissed the picture and started crying. I could not stop crying. Suddenly I remembered my father's words, which he had learned from Father Fredericks: remember always to stay rooted in faith. I began to pray and ask God for a safe return.

Well, it took me almost two weeks to find out that it was all a well-orchestrated ambush, guided by the Haqqani network which is the hard-core guerrilla fighters in Afghanistan. I guessed that it was my job of being a doctor that might have kept me alive at the time because someone told the Taliban groups there is a female American doctor working with US Marines who tried to help our women for better education and health. Also, they were told that I know the local language.

I was sure that my family was very worried about me because they don't know if I was alive or dead or what happened to me. In the meantime, everybody was doing their best to find me.

After about two weeks, I was told about an injured Taliban fighter that needed medical attention. So I was unchained and taken to a nearby Afghan hideout. I was eventually brought to the injured Taliban fighter. I noticed right away that he had a broken leg, a smashed hand, and was bleeding from an injury along his neck. I told my captors that the man would need to be hospitalized. To my surprise, someone spoke in Persian, which was her father's language. When I asked him, "How did you learn the Persian language?" He replied that he used to work in Iran. Later on, I found out from him that it was all an orchestrated plan to capture me. In the meantime, I did what I could for the injured Taliban fighter. He was very surprised to see me work on him so diligently. He asked me, "Why do you do it?" I simply replied, "I am a doctor. My job is to save lives, not take them." This made the Afghan fighter look at me in a puzzled way, and I could see that he was thinking very deeply. Then, he uttered, I never knew that a woman could be so … wise.

Days, weeks, and months soon passed by. I became adjusted to the routine and way of life of helping others. Despite being closely watched and guarded, I came up with a plan to escape. I began to use my charms and became friends with the local kids, especially when they come for help or for medical needs.

Once my ankle healed, I was able to walk with a cane. However, my captors demanded that I wear a *burqa* and be fully clothed with Afghan female garments at all times. This made me feel very uncomfortable. At times, I could not see in front of myself, and many times I would fall down. Of course, the Afghan children would always tease me and laugh. They called me the foreign blind eye who could not see in front of me.

Another problem was the local language, which was Pashto. Although I understood some of it, I began to learn to speak it on my own. Pashto is one of the two official languages of Afghanistan, along with Dari. Since the early eighteenth century, all the kings of Afghanistan were ethnic Pashtuns.

Over a period of about two months, I was able to learn basic Pashto and start making friends with local woman and children. A big problem was that many women did not have basic medical necessities. So a simple cold or other sickness such as diarrhea would turn into a life-threatening disease. Luckily, I had my medical backpack with me when I was captured by the Taliban. However, the supplies in this were limited which forced me to be frugal.

In the meantime, I was constantly trying to figure out how I could send a message out to the nearby outpost United States or NATO ally bases regarding my well-being. I came up with the idea to make a small toy doll made out of hay. It also had parts from my US Navy camouflage uniform which I was allowed to keep. I had learned this trade through my time in the Girl Scout. The final product looked more like a small scarecrow doll; funny but meaningful.

Meanwhile, I was confronted by a Taliban fighter and told that I would have to make a video message. At first, I refused, and I was beaten repeatedly and threatened with rape. Realizing I had no choice, I gave in and decide to make the video message. As the cameras started to roll, I reacted quickly. I was able to run up to the camera, which was sitting on a tripod, and grab it and with my entire strength, throwing it violently onto the ground, smashing it into pieces. Then I began laughing hysterically, realizing that they could not get their way. The Taliban fighters became enraged, and they attacked me. They beat me until I lost consciousness. Then I was placed back into confinement. It would take another month or so before I would be able to be free again. The next time came when one of the wives of the Taliban fighters got very sick and requested my help. So once again, my medical skills helped me.

Regarding my freedom and exchange with other Taliban, they are at Guantánamo Bay, which is the US prison located in Cuba. So one day they came, and they told me I have to do these things. Of course, I refused and so they beat me. They put me on the ground lying on my back. Then they elevated my feet and tied them to a stick, shoulder width apart. This leaves both of my feet entirely exposed. One of the soldiers began beating my feet with a stick. The beating was so bad that I passed out. Luckily for me, when the Taliban leader showed up and asked what happened, he disciplined the Taliban soldier who beat me because they want no harm to come to me. Instead, they have other plans for me. Also, they wanted to know how is it that I know their language. Of course, I did not want to mention that I was Iranian/American because of fear of retaliation. Also, I was aware that the majority of Iranians are Shia Muslims. I quickly realized an answer I learned in the University. And basically dodged a bullet. My head is spinning a thousand times a second, contemplating how will I get out of here.

CHAPTER 22

Unwanted Desire and Captivity

"Whatever makes an impression on the heart seems lovely in the eye."

After several days of captivity, Farah found herself being taken to the warlord leader, Moullah Mehsud. She was in pain and agony due to the severe beating she had received at the hands of Moullah Sardar, who is Moullah Mehsud's eldest son because he discovered her plot to attempt a rescue. Also, Farah felt guilty for her friend who was beaten severely and had her ear sliced off, humiliating her in public.

When Moullah Mehsud saw the poor condition that Farah was in, he became enraged. He approached his son and marched him to the front of a standing crowd. In front of everyone, he slapped him several times in the face. Then he tore down a branch from a nearby tree and began beating Moullah Sardar on his legs and back. In a loud and angry voice, he shouted, "I forbid you to come back to the village until further notice." With that, he motioned his head and Moullah Sardar was quickly escorted away by his loyal troops to the nearby mountains. Then, to everyone's surprise, Moullah Mehsud ordered some of his men to go to the bazaar in nearby Kuwaiti, Pakistan, and purchase some camel madham. It is a special type of oil ointment used to heal open wounds. After a short while, the men returned with the madham, and Moullah Mehsud applied it to some of Farah

Claire's wounds. Nevertheless, Farah Claire was not really concerned about her injuries anymore. That's because she had learned that she was not too far away from the Pakistan border, nearby the great and notorious mountains of Bora Bora. And with this newfound information, she decided to plan her escape. Unfortunately, something unexpected came up.

It started slowly at first. Farah began to develop nausea and other symptoms, which she discarded as the result of trauma associated with her captivity. Then, a woman in the local community who was simply called Grandma came to visit her one day. During her visit, she looked at Farah and smiled and said, "Please give me your hand." The woman started to massage Farah's hand and made circular motions above it. She brought out some henna from her bag and applied it to Farah's palm. She then made a picture of a large leaf which was connected to a much-smaller leaf. Without even thinking about it, Farah immediately knew what Grandma was implying. Farah felt shocked, sadness, amazement, and fear. Farah realized that there would be serious implications if Grandma was correct—what if she was right? Farah began to wonder if she really was pregnant. At the same time, Farah worried about the unborn child. How can she send a message out regarding a rescue attempt for two people? Afterward, the woman wiped away the images with a ragged cloth and disappeared out of the room.

The next day, Farah got very sick and began throwing up. She was nauseous and became sensitive to everything, especially smells. It was then that she came to realize the truth of what Grandma was trying to reveal to her. Farah knew that she was pregnant. All she kept wondering was out of all that has happened to me, why now? She simultaneously cursed and praised Steve. Still, she was worried about how she was going to explain this to Steve and especially to her captors. This would be an extremely complicated matter for everyone around her.

Hygiene became a serious challenge for Farah. That's because the place she was living in captivity did not have any basic sanitation, including running water. So Farah had to devise her own solutions. She had two boxes of baby wipes and other supplies such as rubbing alcohol and hand sanitizer. In the meantime, she learned to be very clean. Anytime that she went to the bathroom, she would have to be escorted outside by another female guard related to the Taliban leader. She was constantly being watched.

CHAPTER 23

<><><><><><><><><><><><><><><><><><><><><><><><><><><><><><><><><><><><><><><>

Unwanted Love Triangle

"Do not choose for anyone what you do not choose for yourself."

Soon Farah began to realize that there was an unwanted attraction from the warlord and Taliban leader, Moullah Mehsud.

One day, Moullah Mehsud's eldest wife came to visit Farah. When she did, Farah noticed that she would stop and talk to other women in the village. However, on this particular visit, the woman told Farah that she had a message for her. It was from Moullah Mehsud. Apparently, he had asked for her hand in marriage. He wanted her to be his bride for the upcoming Nowruz or first day of spring. This was traditional. But Farah also found out that Moullah Mehsud's third wife, the one who was helping her to get her freedom back, had been killed by the Taliban leader's eldest son. This meant the he needed someone to replace her. Since it was the upcoming season of opium harvesting/trading, Moullah Mehsud decided to follow tradition and marry as soon as possible. Even though it is strongly prohibited to marry a nonbeliever, Moullah Mehsud did not care. He wanted Farah.

Farah thought, perhaps since he spared her life, he expected her to reciprocate in return and accept his offer. All that Farah could think about was, *How am I going to survive this situation?*

Out of nowhere, over the next couple of days, one of the Moullah Sardar's royal Taliban troops along with his wife came and offered some gifts to Farah. The gifts included several scarves and rose-watered perfumes, which are a sign of courtship. Of course, Farah did not know what to think about this. She remembered at one point when Moullah Sardar tried to kill her with his bare hands. But now this? It didn't make any sense. She wondered what was going on, and why she was chosen.

It became clear to Farah Claire from this experience that Moullah Mehsud had developed feelings for her. At the same time, she became aware that Moullah Sardar also showed an interest in her. However, Farah Claire was completely not aware that there is a big plan for her. It was about formulating a trade or deal with US officials for her release. The term is to release several Taliban leaders in custody who had been captured a long time ago and detained in Guantanomo Bay. Farah Claire could not help but wonder what is going to happen to her now.

CHAPTER 24

<><><><><><><><><><><><><><><><><><><><><><><><><><><><><><><>

Ride of Your Life: How to Ride a Black-Headed Donkey While Pregnant

"Patience is bitter, but it has a sweet fruit."

Flashback:

Farah remembered as a child growing up in Virginia. She had the chance to go with her family to a nearby farm that raised horses. When she got there, to her surprise there was also donkeys and ponies. Of course, being a child, she wanted to ride the small ponies.

Back to the present.

Because Farah was successful treating the Taliban fighter, her skills were needed again to treat more wounded fighters. However, this time she would be needed to move to another location which was much farther away.

Farah was tied up and straddled along the black-headed donkey. She was forced to ride to an unknown location in the nearby mountains. Farrah was told that because of her medical skills she was to help three Taliban soldiers who have been injured by their own roadside bombs (IED). The ride was very uncomfortable. Farah tried to talk to the donkey and calm it down because she was pregnant and feared for the health of the unborn child. "Please be gentle on me and don't hurt my baby," Farah said. At times, Farah swore the donkey responded by looking back at her as if to acknowledge her pleadings. At one point, one of the Taliban guards heard her talking and began to yell at her. He came up to Farah and struck her with a stick and shouted, "Who are you talking to? Shut up before I make you suffer even more." They continued to ride into the mountains.

As Farah and the Taliban fighters ascended the mountain, the trail got smaller and smaller, and the winds began to pick up. It also began to get darker. After a while, they had to use lanterns. In addition, Farah's bladder began to give out, and she really needed to go to the bathroom. Her body kept saying you need to go now. But she kept calming herself down and prayed to God for a safe arrival. After what seemed like an eternity, she finally made it to their destination. When she arrived, one of the Taliban fighters had already died. His family was there, crying, begging her to try to bring him back to life. Farah was too shocked, in agony, shivering. She felt immense sorrow for their loss, but there was nothing that she could do. She was immediately released, taken down off the donkey and led to the other two survivors. Looking at their injuries, Farah realized that they were in bad condition, and there was little that she could do. One of them had a shattered skull and badly injured eye. He could not be saved. The other one had both legs blown off and was bleeding badly. She applied a tourniquet to stop the bleeding, and she used her scarf to help. Farah yelled at the Taliban fighters. "These injuries are too serious for me to treat. They have to go to the hospital as soon as possible, or else they are going to die." Immediately, Farah opened her scarf and applied it to his wounds. She was punished severely with a beating while she's trying to give help. The Taliban said to the other soldiers, "Bring us *burqa*." "You need to have your hijab and head scarf at all times. Do you understand?" This situation really highlights how women in Afghanistan have no freedom or self-independence for themselves. Instead of being more concerned about the well-being of the injured soldiers, they were shouting at Farah and other females in the area, "Bring me a *burqa*. Bring this *burqa* for the nonbeliever at once!" Unfortunately, the Taliban fighter with the cutoff legs died because he had loss too much blood. Farah then focused her attention on the one remaining Taliban fighter who was barely alive. Her only choice left was to sever his mangled arm at the shoulder. Farah was about to help out when one of the Taliban soldiers pull out a large machete and cut the arm off the injured Taliban fighter. In the same instant, he grabbed a torch and pushed it into the fighter's open wound. It was such a barbaric act to witness. The Taliban fighter screamed out in agony and then passed out. At that moment, Farah had seen enough, and she passed out too.

When she came to, Farah felt the coolness of a small wet rag on her face. She soon realized it was another female in the room who felt sorry for her and began to clean her face off the injured Taliban fighter's blood, which had splattered on her during the previous encounter.

Farah felt immense pain in her stomach and her lower abdomen. She could not remember when was the last time that she had gone to the bathroom, but she desperately needed to go now. After negotiating with the Taliban guard, she was given permission to go to the bathroom. She had held it in for so long that it hurt inside. As she began to relieve herself with an observing standing Taliban fighter nearby, she began to cry feverishly. She looked up into the sky and said, "Is this what I deserve, Lord?" She wished to be magically transported back home to her loved ones. She could not stop crying, feeling both joy and sadness for her unborn child. She touched her stomach and said, "Please be strong, my baby. Please don't leave me. You are my only hope."

CHAPTER 25

Attempts at Rescue

"If we pay attention, we'd realize that the determining incidents in our lives are ordinary things."

On one occasion, Farah was able to provide medical assistance to the daughter of the third wife of Moullah Mehsud, named Bano Khnoh. The daughter's name was Baran. She was a nine-year-old girl with beautiful hazelnut eyes and soft skin. She also had an incredibly beautiful smile. Unfortunately, due to the unsanitary conditions, she had developed a very bad case of diarrhea. The mother brought Baran to Farah so that she could treat her condition. Later on they become very good and close friends. After a close checkup, Farah gave Baran medicine which healed the infection and made her healthy. Farah then began to learn the local language (Pashtun). Baran helped her by giving her a second-grade book with basic Pashtun alphabet even though this was forbidden for women to learn. Males were the only ones allowed to do this. And to everyone's surprise, Farah was able to communicate with the local village women and children in less than a month's time. Because of this, Farah garnered everyone's trust and became known as the American Lady Healer. However, she also brought more unwanted attention to herself from the Taliban. As a result, many members of the Taliban were reluctant to speak around Farah because they were afraid she would understand and know about their plans.

Several weeks later, out of the blue, Bano Khnoh came to visit Farah with some food. She also brought her daughter, Baran, along. The two of them came into the room, greeted Farah, and kissed her hands. Although Farah felt uncomfortable with this, she allowed them to touch her. Then, the mother spoke aloud saying, "Khonam, American," meaning American woman. "You are like a guardian of Afghan women, and we trust you. You are like my sister. I have a plan to get you free because I don't want you to end up like us. Please follow my daughter right now. I will distract the guards. There is a cell phone that belongs to my stupid husband [Moullah Mehsud]. It is nearby in the next compound. It is located underneath a pillow, and it is not guarded. With the cell phone, you can make a call to your friends for help and rescue. But you must act quickly."

Without any hesitation, Farah followed Baran out of the door and into the darkness. Her heart was pounding furiously, and she began to sweat. As they both made their way to the nearby compound. Farah wondered, *Is this another trick? Can I really trust them?*

A few minutes later, they both arrived at the compound. Baran's cousin, another little girl (Amira), opened the door and led them both to another room. She then quickly ran away into the darkness and disappeared. Baran and Farah had to use a candle to see through the darkness. Once they reached the other room, Baran quickly found the pillow, looked under it, and brought out the cell phone. She immediately gave it to Farah and then left out the door. Farah, with nervous and shaking hands, turned on the cell phone and waited anxiously for it to come on. She began to smile and cry and the same time, talking to herself. Then she wondered, *Who should I call? I don't even have a good number.* Suddenly, she remembered the toll free 800 number to call for emergencies. She quickly dialed it and listened impatiently as the phone rang on the other end. To her surprise, someone answered. Farah began to scream into the phone: "Please help, please help me. My name is Farah Claire, and I am a US Navy Medical Officer who has been captured by the Taliban. Please help me. I am nearby the border of Pakistan." Suddenly, she heard a noise and looked back. To her surprise, there was a loud crashing sound, and in the nearby door came bursting in three Taliban troops rushing into the room including the son of Moullah Mehsud, Moullah Sardar. At that moment, Farah dropped the phone, and her heart stopped. The fear of being killed gripped her entire body. She began to shake and cry. "Please don't hurt me," she heard herself mutter.

Moullah Sardar ordered two Taliban soldiers to get Farah. Immediately, they simultaneously attacked her, one grabbing her by the arm and other grabbing her by the hair. Together, they yanked her out of the room. On the way out the door, Farah could her a foreign accent on the phone. It said, "Please repeat, where are you? Where are you captured? How can we help?" Farah screamed out, but it was too late. The other Taliban soldier struck her in the face, causing her to fall to the ground. Then, with a quick motion, he stomped on the phone, tearing it to pieces. Farah then passed out from the blow.

On the next morning, Farah and the third wife, Bano Khnoh, were roused up and brought out into an open area near a small mosque, which was located in the center of the village. The eldest son of Moullah Mehsud wrote some Arabic words and gave a small speech. He said, "From now on, if anybody tries to help this American nonbeliever woman, they will be punished by being stoned and then executed." With that said, he ordered his men to kill the wife of his father, Bano Khnoh, to make an example for everyone. A soldier then pulled out a machine gun and quickly began to unload it into the horrified woman's body. You could hear her children crying as the bullets ripped apart her body. The other woman shouted, "Don't do this. Please forgive her." But it was too late. The sound of the machine gun echoed throughout the village. Bano Khnoh's blood splattered everyone, and she fell lifeless to the ground, right in front of Farah Claire who had been tied up and forced to witness the event. Then he began to punish Farah Claire. The he ordered his men to beat and punish Farah Claire. For several minutes, Farah did not make any noise to the Moullah Sardar. He was surprise at her toughness. So he ordered his men to beat here even more severely.

When Farah awoke, she looked at Bano Khnoh and noticed her friend had been shot in the head. Blood was pouring down her head from everywhere, and the woman was obviously dead. Farah panicked and started to scream. Then, from a distance, someone yelled, "Moullah Mehsud is coming with his troops." With that, everyone began to scatter.

When Moullah Mehsud arrived on the scene, he demanded to know what was going on. His eldest son told his father the traitor has been killed. Moullah Mehsud became enraged. He ordered his troops to release Farah Claire immediately. They took her to a nearby compound, and he ordered them to treat her wounds immediately. Then, he confronted his son. With much anger is his voice, he said, "Who ordered you to kill my wife?" Before Moullah Sardar could answer, Moullah Mehsud struck him in the face several times with his bare hand. In the next instance, he took out his sidearm, aimed it at his son's foot, and shot him. His son screamed out in pain. Moullah Mehsud then ordered his troops to get him out of his sight. "I forbid you to ever come back to this place. If I ever see you again, I will hang you myself. Take him away." In the meantime, there was a disturbance in the village.

About an hour later, the Taliban's medicine man rushed to Moullah Mehsud's compound and informed him that Farah's injuries were far too severe for normal treatment, and she is in severe pain. Because of the severe injuries she received at his son's hands, Farah would need to obtain some *madham*. Madham is a special type of ointment from a camel that is designed to heal open wounds quickly. If they did not treat her quickly, she will never walk again. Realizing that this would be a severe blow to his plans, he ordered his troops to go to Kowithe City, in Pakistan, to retrieve the treatment. This was the closest place nearby that had this type of medicine available. The medicine man returned to Farah Claire and told her, "Don't worry, we are going to help you." Moullah Mehsud has sent his best troops to retrieve medicine from Kowithe City, in Pakistan. Farah Claire heard what the medicine man had said, but her pain was too much for her to bear and she passed out.

Farah Claire eventually woke up. She found herself in constant pain, but after several weeks, she was able to walk. Also, she had been given Afghan women's clothing, despite the fact that she was a foreigner and this was against the custom. However, there was a fear that she may be discovered by people trying to rescue her. So Moullah Mehsud's wife and several other local women from the village took Farah's military uniform off and replaced it with Afghan clothing including scarves and a dark *burqa*. Farah already had one piece of clothing in her medicine bag.

For several weeks Farah was able to hear helicopters in the distant. Whenever that would happen, everyone in the village would run and hide, especially the Taliban fighters.

On one occasion, when she needed to wash herself due to unsanitary conditions in a nearby lake, she asked for permission from a female guard. She was allowed to clean herself off, but two guards would have to watch. When she heard helicopters coming toward the village, the two male Taliban soldiers ran for cover. Farah decided to take advantage of this event. Immediately, she ran toward an open area and tried to flag down the helicopter by waving a white scarf around in the air. The scarf had been given to the Moullah Mehsud family as a gift. Unfortunately, for Farah, the two Taliban soldiers realized what she was trying to do, and they quickly interrupted her by shooting near her feet with an AK-47. At that moment, she just froze. Then, she was forced to see the helicopters pass her by and head off into the distance and disappear. When the soldiers realized everything was safe, they surrounded Farah and began to beat her. One of them slapped her very hard, and she fell to the ground. She was then dragged off to Moullah Mehsud's compound.

After about a month of captivity, Farah tried to be friends with people around. Unfortunately, no one was allowed to talk to her. As time went by, she later learned that she was a prisoner in a village far away, near the Bora Bora Mountains. Sometimes, Farah could hear helicopters from far away. Unfortunately, she was not able to send a signal to tell them she was being held there as prisoner. Farah realized she was in a very difficult situation because she knew that the American and other coalition forces were looking for her. But she was unable to contact anyone and let them know exactly where she was. If someone could have seen Farah's expression, it would have been one of disappointment, sadness, agony, and helplessness. Farah wondered, *Would a rescue from this horrible place ever come?*

CHAPTER 26

Revenge

"Life is complex. You don't have any person who is nice from the beginning until the end. You don't always have the notion of redemption. The bad people don't always pay."

Moullah Sardar felt humiliated. He could not believe that his very own father had treated him so badly. He wondered, "Why did my father treat me so savagely?" Why did he choose the blonde female infidel over him? "Also, why did he slap me in the face in front of my entire clan? Doesn't he know that this is unacceptable? Why did he have to shoot me in the foot? What is so important about this blonde female infidel?" As he had his medics attend to his wounded foot, Moullah Sardar suddenly realized the answer to his own questions. The blonde female infidel was of value. She could be used for ransom, not just merely as a sex slave. With this realization apparent, Moullah Sardar began to craft a plan to bring her back. He would have his men attack his father's group, creating a diversion. Then, in the midst of the confusion, he would steal the blonde female infidel from under his father's nose and take her for himself. He would use her as leverage. Besides, his father would not expect such a bold move from him. The element of surprise would be on his side. Then Moullah Sardar would have his revenge against his father. He would cause events to come about wherein he would ambush his father and kill him, thereby restoring his respect among the other Taliban groups. It would make him more powerful in the eyes of the other Taliban warlords. So he began to put his plan into motion. In the meantime, without his father's knowledge and in secret, Moullah Sardar gathered more fighters that were loyal to him and began to denounce his father. "He's weak, he's old. We need a new leader. We have to gather our forces and attack the Afghan new government and US forces." With that said, he promised the fighters more opium and more money. The crowd cheered for Moullah Sardar. Finally, Moullah Sardar promised, "We must make the invaders leave our land."

Moullah Sardar began to gather his large Afghan Royal Fighters along with Pakistani Taliban groups. Several days before, he had sent a message to the Pakistani Taliban leaders regarding his father being weak and wanting to marry an American nonbeliever Christian female. In the letter, he indicated that everyone must mobilize and take down his father. He further stated that it would provide valuable benefits for both sides, such as more territory to control and also together they could negotiate with the Americans to release several Afghan and Pakistani/Taliban leaders from Guantanomo Bay. In addition, working together they could set a trap for the Americans while negotiating hostage exchanges.

Afterward, for several days, large groups of Pakistani Taliban fighters were mobilizing. Now, they were coming to add their strength to Moullah Sardar's forces against his father.

In the meantime, Moullah Mehsud's Taliban troops were trying to replenish with more supplies and ammo from the Pakistani side. Of course, the other group found out about his son's plans. Eventually, the two groups clashed, and there was a huge firefight among themselves. Many villagers were afraid about the conflict and got caught up in the fighting. They were completely unaware of the village being cut off from the rest of the area. They were under siege. No one was safe. Immediately, a message had been sent to Moullah Mehsud and his troops. They began mobilizing their own troops and fortified their defenses.

They did not know, meanwhile, that all of this movement and activity was being closely monitored by American and Coalition Forces, which included drones and satellite imagery. As the battle began to unfold, Moullah Sardar could taste his victory. He was informed that his father, along with a large portion of loyal troops, had finally been cornered and were soon to be overtaken. With this latest information, he rushed forward to the scene and saw his father being badly wounded and yanked away. Now his father was bleeding heavily. So he ordered his men to bring his father out into the open so that they could face each other. Then, Moullah Sardar gathered the remaining troops and asked his father's Taliban fighters to join him and his cause. He then told his father, "You are weak and have humiliated all of us and broke your promises. By Sharia Law and Islam rule, you will be executed in public to be an example to others that they should not interfere in the rule of Islam and Taliban ideology." Then, he ordered two of his loyal men to tie his father's hands along with his legs together. His father was then forced to sit down in a bowed position. His father began to plead to his eldest son. "This is wrong. We are Muslim and should fight together against Satan and not each other. I order you and your troops to release me at once. You will be punished by the hands of God." Moulah Sardar ignored his father's pleas. He then took out his machete and spoke in Arabic Allah Arkbar from the Koran. Then, with no hesitation, he decapitated his father's head with one sharp blow from the machete. Moullah Sardar picked up the bloodied head and showed it to the crowd. The crowd began to cheer and said Allah Akbar (God is great) repeatedly.

Then, Moullah Sardar ordered his troops, "Find her, the American doctor, and bring her to me immediately." About fifteen of Moullah Sardar's troops rushed to Farah Claire's hideout and ordered her captors to release her to them. Unfortunately, when they got there, Farah Claire was not to be found. So they ordered the men to return Farah Claire at once. Also they informed them that their leader, Moullah Mehsud, had been executed in public. And now they belong to Moullah Sardar. Still, the troops of Moullah Mehsud did not believe what had been said. So, instead, they told the others to come forward. As soon the Moullah Sardar troops came forward to get Farah Claire, there was a large explosion. And the Moullah Mehsud Royal Troops detonated a large IED, which was set for whoever would come to take the doctor. Of course, with the ensuing explosions from all of the chaos, many of Moullah Sardar's troops had been killed and badly injured and unable to fight. Moullah Mehsud's troops came out and finished off the injured Taliban fighters.

In the same moment, a loud thundering gunfire and explosion came from all directions. Moullah Mehsud troops looked up in the air and in shock saw many American and Coalition Forces helicopters on the horizon, and they were attacking everywhere.

In a state of shock, Moullah Mehsud's troops began to scatter.

Meanwhile, an intense firefight erupted between both sides. Eventually, a large group of Moullah Sardar Royal Taliban including Pakistani Taliban fighters who had come to join his forces were demolished and killed. Eventually, Moullah Sardar and twenty other fighters were sighted by Apache helicopters and killed. A large number of Taliban fighters later on was captured by Afghan National Army (ANA) and Coalition Forces. They were taken into custody to face justice.

CHAPTER 27

◇◇

Miracle Messages from Farah Claire

"Fear not he who makes a lot of fuss; fear he who keeps to himself."

Farah Claire decided she was going to try to get messages out for help. She came up with a clever idea to use her skill of making dolls out of scraps, which she had learned to do in the Virginia Girl Scouts. Since she had formed many friendships with small girls and their mothers in several villages that would come to see her for medical needs, Farah would give the girls toy dolls and tell them to hide it and only use it when they would go to the bazaar with their family. Farah was keenly aware that about the strict rules of Islamic law by the Taliban in the region that prohibits the use any type of toys and dolls, especially Western type, for children.

So Farah made four small scarecrow-type toy dolls for several of the girls in the villages. One little girl's name was Saba, eventually becoming a miracle messenger, whose actions would ultimately lead to Farah Claire being freed from captivity.

Farah Clare had somehow hoped that someone would see the little girl with the strange doll made out of US Marines camouflage/uniform material. This was the only material that Farah had available at the time since she was captured.

Along with each toy, Farah embedded a handwritten note with an SOS message from her for help.

After six months, despite many trips into the area when United States and coalition forces had been searching for Farah, there was no success or sign of Farah Claire.

Farah almost had given up hope until that day when the message was discovered.

Saba and her family would often go to a nearby town that was controlled by Afghan and coalition forces. So Farah gave the doll to Saba and told her to take it with her on her next trip to the market. Farah hoped that by a miracle someone would discover the toy doll made out of camouflage material. And that is exactly what happened.

When Saba and her family was at the bazaar to buy some supplies, one of the coalition forces along the Afghan National Army (ANA) with a local interpreter had been making a routine patrol for safety and security of the town and market. The coalition soldier saw the doll and said this is very unusual. "I don't know any shop that sells any toys and dolls. How is that little girl able to get it?" So then they stopped, and with the help of an Afghan soldier and interpreter, they tried to retrieve the doll from the girl. Did you see that it has an American uniform on it? So the local interpreter along with two Afghan soldiers approached the girl and her family and began asking questions. One of the Afghan soldiers forcefully grabbed the doll from the small girl. The small girl began to cry and tried get the doll back. There was a struggle, with both of them pulling on the doll. Suddenly, it ripped apart and out fell a note to the ground. The interpreter grabbed the note and read it to himself. It said, "Help! I am Farah Claire. I'm a US Navy Medical Officer who has been captured by the Taliban." The date looks about six months ago. "I have given this note to a small girl in a village not too far from my location. Please do not harm this girl or her family. Please reward her. She will know where I am being held. Please come to my rescue. I am injured and require medical assistance."

With this, the interpreter ran hastily toward the coalition forces and showed them the note. Immediately, everyone sprang into action. The Captain of the Coalition forces was notified, and he requested the family be immediately evacuated to a nearby coalition base for safety. The small girl and her family were immediately brought to the base and rewarded. They were given food and shelter along with more toys. The Captain of the Coalition forces then radioed the chain of command and American forces about the discovery of the note from Farah Claire. In the meantime, the captain spoke with the small girl and her family through a local Afghan interpreter. He told them that they would be protected and not to be afraid. He knelt down and faced the small girl and told her, "We are going to give you lots of toys and dolls." The small girl smiled, and the family began to move toward the convoy and was eventually escorted into the base. When they arrived, they gave them money, a safe house, food, and shelter. Later on, they both were flown by helicopter to Kabul Airbase, far away from conflict.

Afterward, the local Afghan interpreter along with another intelligence officer asked the family a series of questions. Where is their village located? Unfortunately, the name of the village was not located on the map. However, the family was able to locate a name of a large village. And that village was located thirty-five kilometers to the north of the Bora Bora Mountains. They gave explicit details of the hideout including how many Taliban fighters were there, how much arms and artillery they had. They said there were about fifty to one hundred fighters at any given time and that the best time to rescue Farah would be after dark which was around 8:00 p.m. when the Taliban would be traveling to other villages for patrol and to gather food and supplies. So the intelligence officer gathered all of the pertinent information and sent it via satellite to the headquarters in Bagram Air Force Base. From there, it was sent to the Pentagon. The Pentagon mobilized all their assets including satellite imagery and was able to produce a very detailed map of the village where Farah Claire was being held captive.

There was a sense of urgency because they were worried that the Taliban spies could be alerted to the plan. A key problem was that the family had been seen leaving with the coalition forces. So this made everyone work harder to initiate a rescue mission as soon as possible.

CHAPTER 28

<><><><><><><><><><><><><><><><><><><><><><><><><><><><><><><><><><><><><><><>

Rescued: Free at Last

"Human rights is a universal standard. It is a component of every religion and every civilization."

The message was sent from the Pentagon to the US Special Operations Command (US Navy Seals, Special Forces, and NATO alliances) for Operation Cobra. In the meantime, the Pentagon contacted Major Steve with the latest photo of Farah Claire. Immediately he was requested to come to Fort Meade, Maryland, for an update. He was instructed to keep everything in secret.

When Major Steve arrived at Fort Meade, he met with his chain of command and requested permission to be somehow assisting the mission or the team. After several days of preparation, the Pentagon accepted Major Steve's request and permitted him to assist the mission. However, there would have to be certain conditions in order to ensure mission integrity. Major Steve could only be there to observe, and he could not be involved or interfere with the rescue team. After this agreement, Major Steve was flown to Germany for a mission briefing along with several Special Ops and Intel. Together, they all had to fly out to Bagram Air Force Base in Afghanistan.

While in Afghanistan, days passed by very slowly. Every hour Major Steve waited impatiently for any small details about the upcoming rescue mission. He could not help it. He had a picture of his wife in one hand and the Bible in another. All that he could do was pray for her safety. Yet he began to become more and more tense. He could not sleep for hours. Finally, the go-ahead was given by the chain of command, and Operation Cobra was initiated.

Major Steve has been informed about this matter and met with the base officials. Several hours later, they all flew out in two Chinook Helicopters to Camp Delta at Kabul. After they landed, they immediately met with the Special Forces Commander and then got meet with the rest of the rescue team. The team included US Navy Seals, US Army Special Forces, and Coalition Special Forces. Everyone was concentrating on implementing the plan and rescuing Farah Claire. If everything went along as planned, within the next forty-eight hours, Farah Claire would be rescued successfully and would be on her way to the United States. Although, the mission would be very sensitive, many different aspects would have to be done quickly and in secrecy. Still, everyone was both nervous and excited. The war room was alive with excitement, and everyone was motivated. So now in the US Special Forces operation room, all maps, radar, and radio were being monitored closely. Soon they were able to get live feedback from satellite of the village. Also, many drones had been mobilized, to fly at high altitude, to oversee the entire mission. Everyone was looking at the monitor or television for signs of Farah Claire. Hours and hours passed until by 4:00 PM, to everyone's surprise, they saw a female being guarded by four Taliban fighters coming out of a small mud house going or traveling to the other side next to a bigger compound. They were greeted by ten more or so Taliban fighters at the compound. It looks like it had been fortified. So the cameras zoomed in by satellite. Steve was asked, "Can you identify Farah Claire?" The woman was walking with a limp, but Steve knew somehow that it was Farah. However, he asked, "Can someone please provide me with a copy of the image?" With that said, he ran with the photo along with two other Special Ops personnel to grab an interpreter to interview the Afghan man (Ahmad Zahar) from the village. In the meantime, Coalition forces received conflicting messages about Ahmed Zahar involvement in attacks on Coalition Forces and Afghan National Army (ANA). The information said that it is possible that he is a double agent. Interview cautiously.

Steve, along with an Afghan interpreter and two other US Special Ops personnel arrived at Amarza Holding Facility along with his family. He asked, "Can we talk to you?" So he agreed. And they go with them. In the room, they asked, "Can you please look at this picture and examine this? Is this my wife? Is this my wife?" he asked again. Then, he looked back at the interpreter and told him please tell him to look at the image and confirm this. To everyone's surprise, Ahmed Zahar stayed quiet. After several minutes, he looked at Steve's eyes. "Can I get my reward? I want to go home." But the interpreter responded that he would be more helpful if would kindly confirm. "Then we will give you more money." When it was translated back to Steve, Steve took his wallet out and pulled out all his cash and then thrust it into the lap of Ahmed Zahar. Feeling satisfied, his face changed, and he began to smile. He said, "Yes, that is Farah Claire, the American doctor."

Steve ran back to the command post and told the chain of command, "Yes, we confirm. That's her."

Then two Intel Ops Officers approached Steve and showed them the message from outpost at Helmand Province. It says: Possible double agent and IED maker and facilitator has been seen in the area in which coalition forces and ANA are being attacked.

Steve was confused. He had two conflicting messages at one time. He had fear of safety of the entire operation of mission and his military colleagues. With that said, the commander of the operation gave a green light. And the mission began.

Steve pointed at the monitor and said that's her. He began to cry because he had not seen her for so long. Everyone began to cheer, but the hard part was just the beginning. However, Steve noticed something very odd about the images on the screen. First, the woman on the screen took off her *burqa* and then quickly looked up into the sky. Steve yelled, "Zoom in, zoom in on image Q2." Immediately, the satellite zoomed to a picture. Now everyone could see clearly ... it was Farah Claire. Steve smiled through his tears and realized that Farah was sending them a message. It looks like she had been doing this on purpose, hoping to alert the satellite for help.

Steve noticed on the other monitor something very unusual happening. It appeared that there was a very large group of Taliban fighters that were in the process of surrounding the village. Why, he wondered, is that group surrounding its own people? He didn't have enough time to think about this because now with all of the available intelligence, the word was given to hold the mission. Check all radio monitoring for being supervised. Steve, along with everyone else, was forced to wait.

The Special Forces Unit along with the Coalition forces were ready. They included two Chinook Helicopters and four Black Hawks as escort. Also, there was one Apache Helicopter. The team of fifty men altogether had been briefed and ready to go. Yet they had to wait.

Meanwhile, at the request of the Special Operations Officer, Ahmed Zahar had been authorized to go to the area with the team. He would be needed to identify which house Farah Claire was being held captive. Although, Ahmed Zahar was not aware that he was being watched carefully and his cover had been blown. But only a few mission personnel had been notified about this particular aspect of the mission. Especially, the sniper. Now with that said, they knew that they would have to be ready for anything, including a possible Taliban ambush.

The first go was at 6:45 PM. They got to the helicopters. Then, just as they were preparing for liftoff, a message was sent to cancel the mission: No Go. The weather was not cooperating, and there was the moonlight, which would expose the team. So they all had to wait for complete darkness. Everyone was placed on standby.

The second attempt occurred at 8:55 PM. And the same thing occurred. Then, on the third attempt, around 2:00 AM, there was some movement on the monitors by Taliban forces indicating they are fighting among themselves. The chain of command decided it is a good time to go ahead due to confusion of the Taliban fighters. Immediately, all of the Special Forces Units raced to their helicopters. Given the green light, all of the helicopters proceeded to take off in unison. It took about forty five minutes to get to the site.

The one Apache Helicopter along with two Black Hawk helicopters began to maneuver. All three helicopters began shooting at the Taliban fighters. In the meantime, the two Chinook Helicopters landed safely about one kilometer away. Immediately, all Special Forces crew raced out into the darkness, along with a team with Ahmed Zahar. There was no resistance at this point, because the Taliban were hiding. As soon as the Special Forces arrived at the village, they formed into four teams, Alpha, Bravo, Charlie, and Delta. One goes to fight; the other goes to the rescue. The remaining two teams would be responsible for surrounding the village and providing cover and backup.

The Alpha team along with Ahmed Zahar was now at the center of the village. They asked Ahmed Zahar to guide them to Farah. So Ahmed Zahar took the team to a narrow part of the village. Close to Farah Claire's hideout approximately one thousand yards, he stopped and told the team, "Please stay here while I go check on the guard. If I shake my head, it means she's there. Otherwise, she is not there." With that said, Ahmed Zahar began to run briskly toward the small mud house. This made the team nervous and wondering what's going on. The team scrambled over the radio to inform about Ahmed Zahar running. The Team Commander immediately advised a sniper to keep close eyes on the subject.

When Ahmed Zahar came near the small mud house, he began to shout out in a loud voice, "Kill the doctor. Americans are here." Immediately, two Taliban fighters came out to see what is going on. The interpreter told the team Ahmed Zahar has blown our cover. We have to take him out. Farah Claire's life is in danger because he is telling the Taliban fighters to kill her. With that said, immediately a sniper took down Ahmed Zahar, and the other threw a grenade. There was a large and loud explosion. Then a firefight erupted. It lasted almost thirty to forty-five minutes. Still, the team was able to advance and get to the small mud house. After entering the room, they found Farah Claire wearing Afghan clothing behind a small wooden box, shivering and crying.

In the meantime, the Bravo team, that were fighting alongside the coalition forces, began to engage the Taliban. This gave cover to the Alpha team so that they would be able to take Farah Claire out of the area more quickly.

The Charlie and Delta teams rushed directly into combat and began to engage the other Taliban fighters. A team of six men located Farah Claire's hideout and began yelling. Two Taliban fighters on top of the compound began to shoot at the coalition forces. Both of them were taken out by the Special Forces snipers.

In addition to the above, the Afghan National Army (ANA) coordinated a separate attack along with the US Army against the remaining Taliban fighters in the area. The combined forces together created a good opportunity for the rescue mission to succeed.

Farah awoke to the sound of gunfire and explosions. Only it was not coming from her captors; it was coming from nearby, just outside in the surrounding meadows. Immediately, all of the Taliban fighters reacted and ran out of the room, except two who stayed with Farah. One pointed his gun at Farah and yelled, "Don't move. Don't say anything or I will kill you."

The Taliban was then fighting with the US Commanders in close combat, face-to-face; all has been taken out.

In the chaos, the commandos threw two smoke canisters and one flashbang (stun) grenade at Farah's hideout. This made the remaining Taliban fighters in the room disoriented and confused. In that moment, the commandos entered the room and took out both of the Taliban.

Then, there was a loud explosion. And quiet. Farah did not know what to think. She was terrified. So she rolled herself behind a small wooden box and began shivering and crying, not sure what to do. She was worried about herself and her unborn child. She experienced pain and agony because there was a loud ringing sound in her ears. In addition, there was blinding smoke covering the room. She did not know what to do.

Then she heard it. Someone was shouting, "Farah Claire? Farah Claire? Where are you?" Before she could utter an answer, a soldier was standing over her. He took off his helmet so that Farah could see him better.

A flashlight blinded Farah Claire's eyes, then suddenly she heard a voice. "Are you Farah Claire?" the voice said. Then Farah Claire shook her head and said, "Yes, I am Farah Claire, please help me."

Then, the Commando said, "We're United States soldiers, and we're here to protect you and take you home."

Farah did not know what to say; she was still too afraid to even think, so she said the first thing that popped into her head.

"Thank you for coming back for me."

She shook and quivered as the commandos lifted her up and carried her out. The first commando gripped her hand. "I'm hurt," Farah told them. "Please put me down. I cannot stand or even walk because I am pregnant and in severe pain." Alpha team immediately radioed to the Bravo team: "We need backup with a stretcher. The package needs medical assistance."

The Bravo team radioed back, "Be advised, a team of six along with a medic is on the way to you. Please put out a green chem/light stick so that they will be able to see you."

Unfortunately, some of the remaining Taliban fighters began to advance near Farah Claire's hideout. They began to mobilize and started shooting with small firearms and RPGs. Luckily, the RPGs hit the second mud house. Then, several Special Ops commandos returned fire, killing four, including the person who launched the RPGs. Then, the commandos threw several grenades and killed the remaining Taliban fighters. After several minutes, everything became calm. However, you could still hear several firefights and intense explosions nearby.

Farah Claire so desperately wanted to be able to see their uniforms, to see them better, their faces, to make sure that it wasn't all some bad dream.

The Bravo team arrived at Farah Claire's hideout. Immediately, everyone went to work. First, they put Farah Claire into a stretcher and lightly strapped her in. One of the commandos opened his body's armored vest and gently put it around Farah. He spoke to Farah and said, "You and your child will be protected. I can promise you that." With that said, the team began to move. They began to run out of the house and into the village. The objective was for them to be able to get to the landing zone as soon as possible. As they ran, the other teams began to provide cover for safe passage.

Meanwhile, one of the commandos then reached into his shoulder and ripped a patch from his uniform and pressed it into Farah's free hand.

Once they reached the landing zone, they laid her, gently but quickly, on a stretcher and carried her to a waiting helicopter. Farah heard the hateful sound of gunfire, but it was hard to tell how close it was because of the noise coming from the rotors. There was a lot of explosions, gunfire, and noises coming from everywhere. Meanwhile, the team rushed to the landing zone, making contact with the other teams to cover them. "We have the package," they said, "and we are coming up."

The 2nd, 3rd, and 4th teams had to provide cover fire from side to side to make sure that the other team with the package could pass through safely. In the meantime, Farah Claire could see in the distant the green light coming from the interior of the Chinook Helicopter. Everything was happening so quickly.

And then she noticed the giant Chinook helicopter. The team was getting closer and closer until she can see a lot of American and Coalition Special Ops around two helicopters waiting for Farah Claire and the rescue team.

In an instant, she felt herself being lifted up, into the helicopter. Loud cheers could be heard all around her.

The helicopter lifted off, its rotor blades slicing through the dark.

Okay, this is real. This is real, thought Farah. *I'm going home.*

Once the helicopter was in the air safely, the medic team members began to go to work on Farah Claire. They assessed the situation, making sure that she was okay. They placed headphones over her ears. So now she can hear and send messages to the command post regarding her situation. At the same time, she was told to please stand by. She heard a cracking sound and then a familiar voice. "Stand by, Major Steve, go ahead you can talk to your wife now." With tears of joy in her eyes, she heard Steve for the first time. "Farah, are you all right? Can you hear me? Please respond if you can." Farah was shocked, crying, and smiling and shaking. The commander of the team, seeing that Farah was unable to answer, responded, "Major, don't worry, we have her and she is safe. We will be there shortly. Please stand by." Now Farah was free.

CHAPTER 29

◇◇

Miracle Birth:
A Gift from Farah Claire

"I wish I could show you when you are lonely,
or in darkness the astonishing light of your own
being."

When all of the helicopters landed safely at Bagram Air Force Base, a team of doctors along with ambulances were waiting for the package. When she arrived, she was immediately placed into the ambulance and transported to Bagram Air Force Base hospital. In the hospital, the doctors began a series of checks. They also gave Farah medication to sedate her and make her sleep comfortably. Now, Major Steve, along with the Base Commander arrived at the hospital and assessed the situation. Steve could not contain his emotions. He held Farah's hand to his heart and said, "Farah, you are home." By the next morning, there was a C-17 aircraft ready to take off along with the medical team, and Farah Claire as a patient. After a long six-hour flight, the aircraft landed safely in Germany at Ramstein Airbase. At the base, a large media group had gathered in the terminal for a glimpse of Farah Claire. The news had spread too fast regarding a US Navy female POW who had been rescued by US Special Forces from the Taliban. This had become the number one news story around the world about the successful US and Coalition Forces rescue operation.

CHAPTER 30

<><><><><><><><><><><><><><><><><><><><><><><><><><><><><><><><><><><><><><>

Normal?

"It's not some big event that creates the drama.
It's the little things of everyday life that bring
about that drama."

Steve was at Farah's side during most of the flight. Now that
there was some quiet time, he wanted to spend it talking to Farah.
There was so much to discuss. He really needed to talk to her about
recent events, especially now that she was pregnant. However, he realized that she had been through a terrible ordeal, but now was not the
right time. Also, the doctors had advised that Farah needed several
weeks to recover from her ordeal and go through the healing/recov-
ery process. In addition, they were worried about the baby because
Farah was complaining about a lot of pain in her abdomen area. The
doctors suggested that Farah may need to have a C-section birth and
that as a result the baby would probably be born premature. Steve
had been warned by the doctors that if the baby was premature, it
would have a 60/40 chance of survival. In the meantime, all that
Steve could do now is pray while Farah was sedated.

When the aircraft arrived at Ramstein Air Base, the medical team help evacuated all of the injured soldiers including Farah
Claire. All of the patients were taken immediately to the hospital for
evaluation.

Eventually, all of the patients were transported to Landstuhl Military Hospital. Of course, there was a lot of media now that had assembled at Landstuhl. Everyone wanted to try to get a glimpse of Farah. The hospital was overwhelmed with tight security.

Due to security concerns, the medical team separated Farah and Steve into a more private area of the hospital. Doctors immediately took Farah to an Intensive Care Unit (ICU) where she would be provided with the best medical care possible.

The doctors were concerned about her cleanliness. So they had to remove all of her dirty clothing and replace it with cleaner ones. In addition, they had to shave her head because they had discovered that it was infected with lice. Many nurses helped clean Farah, and for the first time in many months, she was happy, feeling joyful and crying. Steve was impressed with all of the support from everyone involved.

In the meantime, Farah was given several immunizations. She was also given a complete medical exam which included an MRI brain scan, X-rays, and several blood tests. In the end, the doctors decided that Farah's condition was dire, and she needed a medical C-section because the baby could not survive any longer.

After the C-section was preformed successfully, the baby was put into an incubator, and Steve and Farah had to wait at least forty-eight hours before they would be able to hold the baby. Farah was unconscious due to the surgery, but Steve was always there. They were now the proud parents of a beautiful baby girl. They already knew what to name her … Artemisia—in the memory of the late big sister.

Meanwhile, a US delegation team was created, and they arrived at the hospital. The purpose of the team was to investigate the circumstances surrounding Farah Claire's capture and rescue. At the same time, several Pentagon officials had arrived at the hospital. They wanted to control the media attention and also debrief and prepare Farah and Steve for the eventual media frenzy that was about to happen.

About a week later, Farah Claire's family began to arrive. They were provided with transportation and security. However, this did not prevent the media from surrounding them. It was a media circus, with every news agency vying to get the story about Farah.

The family conducted a small news conference at the airport which was assisted by several airport representatives. The family said they were grateful for all of the individuals responsible for bringing Farah back to safety and helping her to overcome her ordeal. They thanked the US Special Forces rescue team, all of the medical personnel, and the support of the American public. In addition, they thanked the people of Germany for their kindness. With that, the family was escorted by the German police and departed to the hospital.

When the family arrived at the hospital, they were immediately taken to Farah's section. Steve met with the family, and together they went to Farah's section. In the hallway, many flowers and posters had been sent to Farah from all over the world. All of the family was greeted by numerous nurses, doctors, and US officials. Finally, the family was allowed to visit Farah. At the first glimpse, they saw a young woman with a shaved head and several IVs and monitors connected to a frail woman who looked like their daughter. Farah had become so small and tiny, and she had lost a lot of weight. Despite this, the family was overwhelmed with joy and happiness at the sight of Farah who was alive.

After some time, everyone was wondering where Steve was. Within minutes, Steve appeared with some flowers and balloons. He hugged the parents and said, "I want to be the first to give you the good news." Of course, they were wondering what he was talking about. Then Steve said, "Congratulations, you are grandparents of a new baby girl." And with that, he hugged and kissed them both. Everyone erupted with laughter and tears of joy. As the nurses and doctors watched the family celebrate, they all began to cry and laugh too. It was a joyous moment.

Several hours later, Farah awoke. Because it was late, the family had left, and were placed in a nearby private hotel. Steve gradually told Farah everything that had occurred over the past couple of days. Farah was elated to learn that she had given birth to a baby girl. She wanted so desperately to see the baby but was told that she would have to wait until tomorrow. Farah was feeling very happy, relieved, and satisfied. When Steve told her that her family was also nearby, she became even more elated.

CHAPTER 31

<><><><><><><><><><><><><><><><><><><><><><><><><><><><><><><><><><><><>

Home Sweet Home?

"If all you ever do is shine your light into the world, that would be enough."

Farah was home now. Everything was fine now, right? No ... not really.

Farah had experienced a very long period of extended absence from comfort, security, her family, and breaks. She had spent seven months on deployment. That means months where she had to deal with the same people day, after day, after day. There is no change, and there is no break. You work with them, you eat with them, and you live with them. If you can't stand them, oh well. If your boss is a jerk or a psycho, there isn't even the escape of going home at the end of the day or having a weekend. Of course, since Farah was in the military, she had to consider the war side of things. In the best case scenario, you are under the constant threat of surprise attacks which can come from car bombs, roadside bombs, suicide bombers, and mortars. Looking at people, who you can see, everywhere, absolutely hate you. In the worst-case scenario, you actually fight. You might kill people. You might lose friends. This would really suck for a few short periods of intense violence during war. However, imagine it sucking for months and months of a slow drone and a psychological beating. That's what Farah experienced.

And then she came home.

At first, she was elated to come home, to see her husband and be with her newborn daughter, and especially to be together again with all of her family and friends. For her, it was a high that can't be expressed very accurately. In a way, she was doing things that she had done many times before, but it had been so long that it felt completely foreign to her. When she first saw her husband, Steve, he was unfamiliar to her. And when she first held her newborn daughter, it felt awkward. Yet, somehow, things were … different.

CHAPTER 32

◇◇

PTSD: The Invisible Wounds of War

"Have patience. All things are difficult before they become easy."

Farah didn't know what the trigger was, but it hit her hard. One day she was lying in bed when she felt a tightness in her chest. Then she could not breathe. She felt closed in and panicky. She bolted upright in the bed, thinking that she was dying.

Maybe it was the young soldier, a woman who had become a POW, who had been beaten and tortured. Maybe it was the faces of all the children that she saw while deployed in Afghanistan. Maybe it was because of the memory of Banko Knowh who had been shot dead in front of her own eyes, seeing the blood splatter and watching the woman die in her own pool of blood.

Even though Farah was home now, she never left the battle-field ... not really. That's because she brought the war home; and it took a toll on her, her family, and her husband. Farah got to be good friends with Jim and Jack. You may know them more commonly referred to as Mr. Bean and Mr. Daniels.

Farah did not want to get close to her newborn daughter for fear that she may get deployed again. Yet despite this fear, a big piece of her wanted to go back to battle because the battlefield made sense. Coming home to dirty diapers, television, and the mundane of everyday life did not. Also, Farah realized that even though she was back home, a bigger piece of her did not want to come back home again.

The home that Farah came back to was not the one that she had left. Her family was not the same. She was not the same. Farah felt that something important was stolen from her, yet there was nobody she could talk to about it. Nobody, except the fellow comrades she was deployed over there with. Oftentimes, Farah would look for combat patches, look for her buddies to talk to, look for the marines and soldiers who went through what she had went through and felt the same way as she did. Farah knew that there were many of them. Many people whose experiences were very different but who had one thing in common. They all felt different, but they were not crazy or had some defective genetic failing.

Sometimes, it was very hard for Farah to come to terms with all the death, destruction, and pain that she had participated in and witnessed. Of course, like most of her comrades, Farah was extremely reluctant about "officially" talking to someone. Even if she needed help, she would not go to it because she thought and knew that the leadership would use that against her for assignments and promotions.

In the end, Farah felt she was alone. She felt trapped in her own memories, sometimes trying to ignore them and oftentimes not being able to. Sometimes she was not comfortable lying in her own bed. Instead, she would climb out of it, and crawl underneath, and curl up into a ball and go to sleep. At other times, she would go outside and lie down under a tree. She desperately wanted the nightmares and flashbacks to stop. The nightmares and flashbacks were so real that she thought she was still being chased by the Taliban and would often wake up in a pool of sweat. She could hear gunfire, explosions, screaming, and chaos everywhere. In the meantime, she watched as the suicide numbers for people like her went up and are still going up.

The military leadership had tried and was trying to change this trend and is having some success. Despite this, Farah wondered sometimes if the world, especially her family, would have been better off without her.

Yet for soldiers like Farah with PTSD, she often felt the very act of seeking help from mental health professionals could be information that could be used against her, to target her, and make her feel like she was a burden to the system. Indeed, Farah felt that way, and she was afraid to get the help that she needed. Farah also feared that the problem may be made worse with the so-called discovery of a PTSD gene. If the data is used in the wrong way or misinterpreted, people like her with PTSD now would be considered genetically dysfunctional.

So instead of being a burden to the Navy, Farah ended up being a burden to the most important people in her life, her husband and child. Fearing being minimized as a soldier, Farah, like so many others, went underground. It seemed the very thing that leadership was using to try to help her actually worked against her.

Whenever Farah would close her eyes at night, sometimes she would still see herself back in Afghanistan, captured as a POW, wounded, helpless, seeing herself picking up the body parts of fellow marines or soldiers. She still sees herself holding fellow marines as they die in her arms or on the battlefield. She can still see the blood of Afghanistan children spattered over her uniform as they take their last breaths due to no fault of their own. In the quiet moments of the day, when she is alone with her family, she sees the many faces of all of the wives, children, husbands, mothers, and fathers whose lives she, in some ironic way, destroyed.

Farah's mind tells her that she did not cause their pain and grief. However, her heart tells her otherwise. She knows that she cannot change their pain but realizes she can change hers and the pain that she inflicted on her family due to war. Of course, only a marine or soldier understands that physically being home doesn't mean coming home.

Coming home from battle seemed to be one of the easiest things to do. It seemed that you just get on a plane. Yet after spending hours, weeks, and months getting help and talking to someone about her wounds, Farah is only beginning to understand how to come home.

Farah is, by military culture, what some would identify as a broken or deadwood marine or soldier. Although she does have wounds from war, her wounds are the invisible kind, the type we bear in our souls. Farah is not ashamed of them. Because for her, and many others like her, they are just as real as the ones that bleed.

With the help of her husband, Steve, Farah gradually learned to overcome her PTSD. She successfully completed the twelve-step program for recovering alcoholics and is no longer addicted to alcohol. Also, she has become much more involved with religious activities, going to church and professing a life of Christianity. Because of her parents' influence, she is now an advocate for bringing others to Christ. In addition, she is an active participant in group therapy through the VA Hospital program. Oftentimes, she volunteers to speak at groups where she can talk openly in public to veterans, especially those from the Vietnam era. After a long recovery, she has returned to her roots, performing as a doctor in her practice of medicine. She has become a symbol of hope and determination.

Finally, after so many requests from the public, Farah decided to go public with her story. She made the rounds on CNN, Fox News, and other various talk shows including *Oprah* and the Tyra Banks's show. This provided Farah some sense of healing. Yet she knew that it was only half of the solution. The other half of her healing would involve her having to do something that she knew would be difficult … going back. Farah knew and believed that the only way she could heal completely is by going back and helping the innocent women and children of the war. This is what she felt in the deepest part of her soul.

CHAPTER 33

<><><><><><><><><><><><><><><><><><><><><><><><><><><><><><><><><><><><>

Why Do You Want to Go Back?

"There is much hope in hopelessness; for at the
end of the dark night, there is light."

Why do you want to go back?

That seems like a simple question. But it is a loaded one. Why
would *anyone* want to go back to a conflict, let alone one that has
been raging for almost ten years, first as front-page news and now as a
side story to political discussion about the national debt? Why would
any sane person want to return to risk life and limb in a war that has
no clear objective and faltering popular support?

Why does anyone want to go back to IEDs, rockets, machine
guns, explosions in the middle of the night, long hours, brutal desert
sun, icy winter winds, long marches under heavy packs, endless hours
of tedium, boredom, pointless work details, angry locals, children
with outstretched hands begging for pens or water, crappy food, no
sleep, sand in every crevice, overbearing officers, fragos, rude POGs,
messed-up paperwork, ambiguous letters from lovers, poor leadership, missed birthdays, missed graduations, missed parties, lost jobs,
failed businesses, lost opportunity, broken hearts, unemployment,
alcoholism, depression, and post-traumatic stress disorder?

How, when faced with the choice to deploy again or to get out
and live a comparably soft civilian life with all the comforts Western

civilization and its opulence can offer, does a veteran choose the former?

Why do you want to go back?

The question hangs in the air, floating like a wisp of smoke over the sounds of children playing kickball, the hissing of freshly opened beers and the soft wind. If anyone is listening to the conversation, they will get extra quiet for a moment to hear the secret. Because there has to be a secret, if someone is going to go back to a war, a thing on the surface so noble (but so foolish), to justify another year without friends and family and several years to follow of cold conversations and uncomfortable, averted eyes that say let's change the subject.

When someone asks, I realize that I have about thirty seconds to condense years of frustration, painful memories, self-justifications, introspection, conversations with comrades, insecurity, guilt, resentment, and humble prayers into an answer that is honest and accessible. Because the moment I open my mouth, interest and comfort begin to wane.

When I start to speak, I am weighed down by all of this.

How can I say that I would feel guilty if I did not go or, even the full truth, I would hate myself if I did not go again, to someone who has never worn combat boots? How can I make a statement about my own choices about war, risk, sacrifice, and death, without making an inherent value judgment about their own?

I have taken to saying that I am going back because "chicks dig the uniform." It is simpler that way.

How do I tell people that I do not want to look back on my generation's legacy and see the wreckage of a self-absorbed Facebook culture? How can I say that I often feel alone when in bars and surrounded by people, and when we talk about our petty concerns, I feel hollow and angry at myself for not being in the fight?

How can I not come across as some self-righteous, look-at-me jerk?

Am I that jerk?

How can I explain the hours I have spent watching or reading the news, seeing video or photographs of men with overloaded packs on their backs, rifles or machine guns in their hands, and a grim weariness etched across their too-young faces, and wanting to be there with them? What sense does that make, especially when here in America I am safe, fat, and (supposedly) happy? How can I think this, knowing how messed up the military can be or how bad my last deployment was? How can I look past a broken promotion system, garrison-centric attitudes, and the ridiculous polices that hamper our war effort?

Are the wars about bringing American-style democracy to the people of Afghanistan? Are they about rooting out Al Qaeda? Are they about putting a McDonald's in Kabul or Baghdad?

I cannot control what our government says this is or is not about. But for me, and for many other veterans of the wars in Iraq and Afghanistan, it is about the job. The job is protecting our nation and protecting one another. It is about experiencing a sense of exhilaration and pride that is unmatched in the civilian world. It is about assuming hardships that most people would not even consider and doing it with a sharp salute and a sense of purpose.

It is about fighting the enemies of our nation. It is about seeing the looks of joy on the faces of our loved ones when we get home. It is about remembering those who went outside the wire (or just went to the chow tent) and did not come back. It is about all of the men and women in the combat support hospitals, in Germany, in Washington, or in Everytown, USA, recovering from or living with the physical and emotional wounds of war.

It is about thousands of people who died in New York City simply because they went to work one Tuesday morning.

It is about seeing a man like Salvatore A. Giunta stand before our president and our nation to receive the highest honor conferred to our fighting men and women, the Medal of Honor, and hearing him give the credit not to himself but to the men who stood with him when everything went to hell.

Why do you want to go back?

I have spent too many moments at work, at school, or by myself in my room with a cold beer in my hand thinking about how difficult it would be to go back. As comfortable as my life is here, I had grown weary of the daily slog of work and feigning interest in polite conversation with people who seemed distant or dishonest about their perspectives on military service.

When I left Afghanistan in 2009, I did my best to forget about how difficult my deployment had been. I had been a combat medical doctor and a translator. I was upset at the military for not supporting our mission (logistically, in personnel, or in any real strategic sense), tolerating corruption, and ignoring its own doctrine. Some people didn't come home (or come home whole) because of poor leadership.

That deployment had left me bitter and angry, and those feelings had stained or ruined relationships with people I loved. I knew that if I had really changed—and I believe I have—then I would have to stop feeling sorry for myself. I would have to do something.

I began to have conversations with old war buddies—usually over a couple of beers—about doing it again. Some of them were angry that I would consider joining back up. A few of the older NCO's were not surprised at all.

I began to exchange news stories, opinion articles, and book suggestions with one of the former platoon leaders of my old company. He was about to assume command of the unit, and he invited me to the change-of-command ceremony.

I showed up at the armory wearing jeans and a hoodie with my hands in my pockets. All around me soldiers worked to prepare the drill hall for the ceremony. It was not long before a few of the veterans of the unit recognized me and began to tease me as they shook my hand.

"Couldn't keep you away, huh, Raab?"

"Get out while you still can, Sarge!"

"I knew you'd be back!"

I answered them with a flurry of gruntspeak: insults, curses, and suggestions on where they could shove any reenlistment contract. To an outsider, this would have seemed like hostility.

It was not.

"Do you want to stand in formation with third platoon?" my old platoon sergeant asked. "We'll make a place for you."

"No, thanks," I said, lying through my teeth.

As the ceremony began, I watched the various platoons form up. I sat with the incoming commander's girlfriend and parents as an "honored guest" where I could not have felt more out of place.

The men snapped to attention, tall and straight, and it was everything I could do not to do the same.

I listened to the speeches of the officers and watched the company guidon pass to the hands of the incoming commander. I knew then that if they were going, I was going to go too. But it had taken me a long time to admit that I couldn't stand by and let them go without me; and it took a lot of thought, a lot of conversations, and a lot of prayer to reach a point where I was okay with risking everything one more time.

Why do you want to go back?

It is about knowing that I traded another year of my prime to go stand and face hardship and the enemy like a woman, faithful, not in politics or policy, but in God and the marines in my platoon. It is about trying to be something more than what our culture tells us is important or cool. It is about shrugging off the anger that sometimes bubbles up when I think about how so few have given so much for so many.

It is about doing something of consequence, if not on the political level, then on the personal. It is about standing alongside, serving with, working for, and leading some of the greatest men that I will ever know, men to whom words like *honor, brotherhood,* and *duty* are said without snickering irony or shame.

Why do you want to go back?

Because I can help. And, in so doing, be helped myself.

CHAPTER 34

◇◇

Triumphant Return

"People first concerns themselves with meeting their basic needs. Only afterwards to they pursue any higher needs."

Farah Claire could not believe it, but it was true. She had returned to Helmand, Afghanistan. She had returned to the very same village in which she had been captured. She felt a sense of exhilaration and happiness.

As soon as she arrived at the village, groups of villagers came out to greet her. She remembered many of the faces, but most were unrecognizable because so much had changed. The village was now safe from the Taliban, and it was growing. Everyone was cheering, and there were smiles and laughter all around. Farah surprised everyone by giving out gifts that she had acquired with the help of the United Nations. To Farah's surprise and amazement, a little girl came up to her and gave her a backpack. It was the same medical backpack that she had taken away from her when she was first captured so many years ago. With tears in her eyes, she thanked the little girl and hugged her.

Farah was shown around the new village. It had become a growing community now. A small clinic had been built to meet the medical needs of the villagers. Farah noticed on top of the clinic that there were many solar panels. It was explained to her that the solar panels help save energy, and the power generated from them helps the clinic to be open for long periods of time. Farah was impressed!

Farah provided the villagers with four new medical backpacks. Each one was filled with up-to-date medicines, immunizations, cotton swabs, gauzes, and other medical supplies. Farah knew that the villagers needed these items, especially to combat diseases which were rampant. Of course, everyone was excited to see such a large number of medical supplies. Now the villagers had a means to fight dysentery, typhoid, and cholera, common problems.

In addition, Farah gave the villagers numerous solar radios and books. The solar radios were easy to use and could be an important source of communication. Many of the villagers enjoyed reading, but books were few and hard to come by after the Taliban destroyed most of the literature. Now that the villagers had their freedom; many desired to pursue education. Farah knew that the books would help the villagers, especially the young children.

Then, Farah gave a short speech to the group. She told them she was thankful to be able to return to their village and that despite the hardship, she was happy to be there. She encouraged everyone to work hard and told them all that foreigners cannot fix the problems with Afghanistan; only Afghanis can make Afghanistan better.

> "Whenever you can, act as a liberator. Freedom, dignity, wealth, these three together constitute the greatest happiness of humanity. If you bequeath all three to your people, their love for you will never die."
> — Cyrus the Great King of Persia

CHAPTER 35

<><><><><><><><><><><><><><><><><><><><><><><><><><><><><><><><><><><><><><>

The Hand of God: A Blessed Legacy

"The night hides a world, but reveals a universe."

We opened a charity in the name of my sister. We call it the House of Artemisia. It was established to help children whose parents have died. It has been very successful, and we devote much of our time to the charity by checking up on the children. Also, we expanded the charity to other parts of the world, such as South Africa and the Philippines, Laos, and Vietnam. For example, we opened a small clinic and school in South Africa and in the Philippines. In addition, I devote my time when possible to work with a team of Doctors without Borders in rural areas like the Middle East, Asia, and Europe. Currently, working near border of Turkey and Syria for refugees. Also, I was in Israel and Jordan to help establish the United Nations Safe Zone. Provided health care, women's nursery. We have a lot of good sponsors from the United States and around the world.

One of our greatest achievements was to get help from the UN/ UNICEF and NATO to establish a refugee camp with solar power. So now refugees can have light and electricity in the camp. We are hoping to be able to expand this.

Another project that we are working on involves teaching refugees, how to utilize and raise their own food and use the biofuel. Currently with the help of other organizations, we are expanding our efforts to Africa, focusing on agriculture. We've been awarded many accolades for these efforts. And all of it is inspired by the death of Artemisia. I'm sure that she would be very proud of our achievements. With the help of the US Air Force which donated the air support to drop food and equipment. They dropped supplies from other countries from Europe and the United States. The Navy contributed with a water purification system. They also donated their time from army engineers and technicians who built bridges, roads, clinic, solar-powered station, wind turbine plants for several villages, water purification systems, and finally, a school and a small church. Our sincerest gratitude is appreciated to all parties that helped out. A big part of the success was the reduction of diseases through vaccinations. With the help and support of our military, especially available resources, doctors, and nurses were instrumental in curtailing diseases through vaccinations.

REFERENCES

- Iran
- Tehran
- Tabriz
- Bazagahan
- Khorramshahr
- Abadan
- Majnun Islands
- Khuzestan
- Fao Peninsula
- Shi'ite Muslims
- Sunni Muslimns
- Iraq
- Burqa
- Evin
- Bagram Air Force Base
- Bora Bora mountains
- Taliban
- Haqqani Network
- Nowruz
- Pashtun
- Dari
- Medevaced
- Moullah
- Ayatollah Khomeni
- Shoshana Johnson
- https://mldoyleauthor.com/books-by-m-l-doyle/excerpts/

- https://www.foxnews.com/world/hell-on-earth-inside-irans-brutal-evin-prison#ixzz2JI0SrLx9
- https://spectator.org/59687_jimmy-carters-legacy-war/
- https://www.encyclopedia.com/history/asia-and-africa/middle-eastern-history/iran-iraq-war
- https://mldoyleauthor.com/books-by-m-l-doyle/excerpts/

CPSIA information can be obtained
at www.ICGtesting.com
Printed in the USA
LVHW020955291221
707428LV00004B/133